COLD OPEN

ANDREW RAYMOND

CHAPTER ONE

Davie Bone clutched his head and groaned as he walked into work at the Govan docks. He felt minging. A resident of Pukesville, Glasgow. Population, one. His head was pounding, his tongue tasted of stale cigarettes, and his whole body ached from the night before. He was fur-tongued. Goosed. Dying. Or so he claimed.

In reality, Davie had no idea what dying truly felt like. It had to be far worse than the aftermath of a mere five pints down The Laurieston on a Wednesday night. At school, Davie had run with the 'bad crowd'. While the others were genuinely violent and scary, Davie just wanted to make the other kids in class laugh. He was badly behaved – shocking, really – but he was never actually 'bad' the way the other boys were.

He had become accustomed to being around the most feared lads in Eastbank High – and that was saying something. The Shettleston school was one of the worst-performing schools in the country. But outside of school, his quick patter seemed juvenile. The Eastbank lads were easily entertained, but a fifty-year-old, sixteen-stone welder from Bridgeton wasn't so easily amused.

The crew from Fallon Construction, contracted for work on the new Govan-Partick bridge, were proper men. Men who could actually grow proper beards. Their stubble could have sanded an oak tree, and all had hands like slabs. By comparison, Davie's hands were like those of a teenage girl beautician.

His patter didn't cut it on site, and it definitely didn't fly on a night out. The only way to earn his colleagues' respect was to keep up with their drinking pace without falling over. Unfortunately, Davie had whitied outside the Laurieston before it was even a new day. To make matters worse, he had attempted to pull the one female on the crew, Fiona McGee. By far and away the hottest woman Davie had ever seen in real life.

Blonde, blue-eyed, she was into kickboxing and weightlifting. Davie had even secretly tracked down her Instagram page one night. Away from the site, she looked like a porn star. But God help anyone at work who ever tried it on. She could handle herself just fine, but her fella at home was a boxer. An actual professional boxer with ties to gangsters. She was the best steel erector – her genuine, official job title – on the Fallon Construction crew. And woe betide anyone who tried to make a joke about it. A mistake that Davie had made once.

And only once.

In the aftermath, Davie had found himself locked in a Portaloo one lunchtime, as Fiona and three men who poured concrete for a living rocked it violently from side to side until the contents of the loo sloshed waist-high over Davie. He happened to find himself working on his own for the rest of that day.

Davie could hear his name being sung in a mocking tone somewhere behind him. A chorus of laughter followed from the group. 'Fuck off, man...' Davie whined to himself in a pathetic tone. His head felt like a bag of chisels. He could really have done without the songs on top of everything else. But by the time his day was done, Davie would look back fondly on the memory of throwing up in front of Fiona McGee and the others at the entrance to the construction site. The memory of being buckled over, his throat going stiff, his mouth hanging open, grimly anticipating the wretched feeling of throwing up for the seventh time that morning, would be like a beautiful dream compared to what was to come.

Fiona shouted, 'Mebbe stick to the McFlurrys next time, Davie boy?' She then patted one of the larger men so hard on the shoulder that he almost stumbled. The foreman, Gerry, was the only one who could keep a crew like that in check. When they assembled in front of the static caravans that comprised the Fallon Construction site offices, Gerry's appeals to lay off young Davie were heeded.

All Davie wanted now was to work with anyone but Fiona. Please lord, don't let him have to work all day right next to her after making such a tit of himself the night before.

Gerry did a double-take when he saw Davie's grey face. 'Chin up, son.' Gerry's was the only sympathetic face on the site. 'You know the best cure for a hangover?'

Davie was almost scared to ask. 'What?'

Gerry couldn't help breaking into laughter before the punchline. 'Seven hours in the pissing rain with a shovel.'

The facade of sympathy broken, Davie took in the cackling faces surrounding him.

Fiona had her arms crossed, unimpressed about having to work with him all day. 'You and me are breaking ground for foundations over there.' She indicated a muddy patch of scrub flecked with occasional grass near the dock's edge, where the

Govan side of the bridge would land. 'I'm on the digger. We've four steel girders to lock in down there by lunchtime.'

One of the scaffolders called out, 'Keep your eyes on her hole, son, and you'll be fine!' He scanned the crowd as laughter broke out, but his good humour didn't last long. Fiona, standing a few feet away, belted him on the back of the head. If there were still a few areas of public life where the #MeToo movement hadn't quite penetrated, it was fair to say that a construction site on a Govan dock was one of them. But Fiona had found that a deftly delivered left hook was the only social media message some of the men there understood.

Gerry raised his hands. 'Right, enough. Let's crack on.'

Davie stared at the ground, wishing it would just swallow him up. Fiona breezed past him towards the digger. 'Pull your socks up.'

'Eh?' Davie said.

'Pull your socks up over your trousers.'

'Whit for?'

'Well, you can wait until the first time you get a rat scuttling up the inside of your trousers if you want. I thought it would be best to warn you now.'

'Rats?'

'Bloody right, rats. The place'll be crawling with them over there once we break ground. Glad I'm in the cab th'day.'

Half an hour in, and Davie and Fiona had made a healthy start on digging out holes for steel foundations. With Fiona helming the digger, Davie was in the hole in the ground with a shovel, pulling out whatever pieces the digger was missing. Rain was lashing down, leaving Davie standing in a rapidly filling puddle, with several rats scurrying in and out of the mud. After the first few sightings, he had made his peace with them. That was the key. When they sensed you panicking and jumping around, causing vibrations, that was when they went into overdrive. Davie found that if he just cracked on with the task at hand, the rats stayed out of his way.

He kept picking away at the south wall, pulling out boulders that were lodged into the side. It needed to be a clean wall for the foundation to be strongest. As he drove his shovel into the wall at the side of the huge rock, he prised the shovel from side to side, teasing the rock out. When it finally popped out, it brought a long, heavy sack of soil with it.

Fiona paused, as Davie stopped work. He tossed his shovel aside. He was bent over, peering into the ground. Fiona moaned to herself, assuming he was about to whitey again. 'Go get some Irn Bru for fuck's sake...'

Then she realised he wasn't being sick. Whatever he was looking at was under the lip of the hole, out of her sight. She was about to climb down out of the cab for a closer look when Davie flung himself back and away from the wall. He let out a terrified yelp, his eyes as big as dinner plates. He threw his arms out to the side, as if needing to hold on to the mud wall behind him to keep himself upright.

He was actually just trying to get as far away from the opposite wall as possible. Now Fiona assumed that he'd uncovered some kind of hellhole warren of rats, particularly as he was now scrambling out of the foundation hole as if his life depended on it. He ran a treadmill of loose soil and mud for a few seconds trying to get out, like some cartoon character's legs running in midair after going off a cliff, and remaining in suspended animation.

Fiona stormed over, ready to give him an earful. 'What the fuck are you–' She stopped in her tracks when she saw it.

Davie was still crawling along the ground, trying to get away.

'Is that...' She began.

Davie didn't have to say a word. They both knew what it was.

Fiona whipped around towards the site offices. She screamed, 'Gerry!'

Inside the static caravan, Gerry threw his pen down and muttered to himself about the interruption.

Then Fiona screamed again. It was unlike any sound she had ever made on the site before. Gerry broke into a frantic run.

When he reached the foundation hole, Davie was on his feet again, standing beside Fiona, staring at a clear plastic bag that had what was clearly a human skeleton inside.

CHAPTER TWO

IT HAD BEEN the same nightmare for the past three nights. After the first two nights, he had almost expected it to return. And normally any time his head filled with images and sounds of his deceased wife Eilidh, it was cause for celebration for DCI John Lomond.

But in this instance, it was unequivocally a nightmare.

Or at least, it started like a dream.

Snippets of memories sitting at her bedside in the maternity unit of the Queen Elizabeth Hospital, listening to their carefully curated Spotify playlist. Holding her hand. Following the breathing they had rehearsed. Each breath bringing their child closer to entering the world.

'Entering the world'. It was a phrase Lomond had heard numerous times throughout Eilidh's pregnancy. But it had felt to him like their child had been a part of the world the moment they found out Eilidh was pregnant.

In the nightmare, those innocent and healthy moments together soon gave way via a violent jump in time, to Eilidh being tended to with great urgency by more doctors than should ever be in one patient's room at a time.

With the entrance of each new doctor, the stakes rose. The worry etched a little deeper on their faces. Progress on stemming Eilidh's bleeding was not going in the right direction.

John looked on helplessly. He pleaded with Eilidh to hang in there.

Then she was rushed into theatre.

A door shut in John's face. For a moment he was left alone.

Then all the frenzy of activity disappeared, and he was standing over Eilidh's lifeless body on a metal table. The instruments of the operation to try and save her and the baby's lives still sitting out.

Her eyes were closed.

So were John's. Still the tears found a way to force their way through.

He couldn't close his eyes tightly enough to stop them.

He gripped her hand, longing to feel some pressure back from hers. As he opened his eyes, he told her – as he had done in real life – 'I'll never love anyone else like you.'

That was always the point at which he woke with a...

"A start" wasn't sufficient.

Chest-heaving panic. Wide-eyed, from lying down to sitting up in a fraction of a second. Gasping for air like someone had been smothering him.

As he regained control of his breathing, he checked the time on his phone.

3.28am.

Shit. Getting back to sleep would be an ordeal now. And if he failed, the rest of the day would be a total write off. He anticipated spending the next hour trying to get back to sleep, as he had done the previous night.

The same thought ploughed over and over in his head. He knew now that there was only one way to silence it.

He tapped out a text message:

"Hi Catriona, it's John. Sorry to message so late/early. But I can't do tonight after all. I'm sorry."

He paused. He wondered about adding some sort of addendum. To leave some ray of light on the table, hinting at possible future encounters. But he dismissed it. He knew that for the nightmares to stop it needed to be a clean break.

He scrolled up to her first message, sent three days earlier.

"Hi John, Isla said it would be all right for me to message you..."

Talking to someone else, even just via messaging felt weird and wrong. But also hopeful. It made him think of the future for once, rather than whatever his current investigation was.

He turned his screen off and set the phone down on the bedside table again.

Then he fell asleep peacefully for the first time in three days. He felt relieved.

It would prove to be only a temporary peace.

WHEN HE WOKE, it wasn't to the sound of his alarm at half past six. He had long since sailed past that.

The sound that woke him was the climax of the *Jaws* theme tune. A ringtone he had recently assigned to his boss, Detective Superintendent Linda Boyle. In his advancing years, Lomond had discovered the entertainment to be found in assigning comedic ringtones to his contacts. Linda was the *Jaws* theme, and had previously been *The Godfather*. He had spent way longer than he should have one night coming up with funny options for the rest of the team, but ultimately concluded that they were really only funny if the other person was around to hear them.

What really startled him though was the time on his phone.

Almost eight o'clock. In Linda's book, practically lunchtime.

In a flap about sleeping in, Lomond answered with a string of apologies.

Linda had to interrupt. 'John, I don't give a monkeys...'

He jumped out of bed and threw the curtains open. He recoiled from even the modest, dull daylight outside.

On the street below was a hearse loaded with a coffin surrounded by flowers.

DEAREST MUMMY was spelled out by one of the arrangements.

Lomond had been to his share of funerals, and the one job that he admired someone doing more than any other was in the funeral game. Everyone has bad days at work and isn't as pleasant or helpful or nice as they could be. But undertakers couldn't afford to have days like those. Every shift, they were dealing with people whose lives were not just shattered. They were still in the process of being shattered.

In a way, detectives and undertakers had a lot in common, as far as Lomond was concerned. They each had become grimly familiar with death on a daily basis, and had a responsibility to the grieving that was uncommon in any other trade.

For most people, buying a flat on Maryhill Road right above a funeral directors' wouldn't exactly appeal. But on the plus side, he was only around the corner from his beloved Partick Thistle's home ground. Not that he ever had time to catch a game. As a DCI the days of the week stop mattering. As the saying at Helen Street police station went, there are only two days of the week: days you work, and days you don't.

Today was the former, but DSU Boyle wasn't going to hold it against him.

'John, you'd better come in,' she explained.

'Fresh one?' he asked.

Linda paused. 'Not exactly.'

CHAPTER THREE

Finding a skeleton buried by the banks of the River Clyde wasn't exactly a regular occurrence for the Helen Street team – or any other team, for that matter. When Lomond arrived at the scene twenty minutes after Linda's call, his expectations were tempered for a number of reasons.

Firstly, it was unlikely they would be able to identify the victim within even the first forty-eight hours, unless they got lucky with a DNA match. But the chances of that were slim. Then there was the time-scale factor. The usual sense of urgency at a crime scene didn't apply there. Forensics can do a sweep of the area for potential evidence, but discovery sites are contaminated by default even if a body is barely cold. The Helen Street team were facing a discovery site possibly over a decade old where construction workers had been pounding heavy machinery around for a few weeks, digging up trenches and piping and foundations. Ordinarily, yellow plastic numbered markers would have been laid on the ground to highlight anything that warranted further examination. If the forensics team had done so at the riverside scene, for the first time they might actually have run out of markers.

There was also the fact that no one on the site needed to be treated with any suspicion. At any other body discovery site, it was always at the back of Lomond's mind if someone present had been involved. There was also no use rushing door to door to check for witnesses of anything suspicious. If anyone had seen anything, it would have been years ago. How many years depended on what Moira McTaggart – Forensic Scene Manager for the Scottish Police Authority – had to tell Lomond.

Until they had an ID, so many of the usual avenues of enquiry would be up in the air.

There would also be unwanted press attention. A skeleton found by the riverside made for easy front pages with shock value. In a missing person's case, the press can be useful, helping jog the memories of potential witnesses who may not even realise they'd seen something important. In the case of a skeleton, all the press had to contribute was macabre speculation.

It was a win-win for the press. Until the remains were identified, pressure could be heaped on the police. And once the identity was made public, the recriminations would swiftly follow. How had the police failed to find the body? Who was to blame?

And then came the most damaging speculation: is the killer still out there?

Detective Sergeant Ross McNair and Detective Inspector Willie Sneddon had been on the scene for half an hour already.

As the only man in Helen Street who could get away with asking in such a way, Willie said, 'What time d'you call this?'

Lomond shook his head. 'A couple of years too late by the sounds of things. What's Moira saying?'

Willie turned to Ross.

Ross flinched. 'What are you looking at me for? You've been senior on site for the past half hour.'

Lomond huffed. 'You mean to tell me neither of you has bothered to talk to the chief forensic about these remains yet.'

Sheepishly, Willie admitted, 'I was waiting for you to deal with her.'

'Christ, Willie...'

'She said she wisnae ready.' Willie leaned in, forcing himself to keep his voice down. 'And you're the only one she's not totally weird with. She freaks me out.'

'That's because you've never bothered to learn how to talk to her.' Lomond looked towards the white forensics tent erected over the hole that Fiona and Davie had dug, dwarfed by the heavy machinery and two cranes towering over the site. White plastic sheeting had been laid down around the edge, but there were no pathologists visible. Along the dockside, further white screens had been erected so that the team from the Scottish Crime Campus could conduct their investigation in private, without anyone across the river being able to see.

Moira popped up from the lip of the hole like a meerkat. She had her paper hood up and was wearing a mask. 'John,' she called out in an unfamiliar tone, lowering her mask. 'I thought I heard you galumphing around.'

She almost sounded...not sullen. Maybe even...happy?

Willie screwed his face up. 'Ga*lumph*ing?' he asked Lomond.

Ross added, 'She seems a bit chirpy this morning.'

'Moira Dreich?' said Willie. 'Surely not.'

Moira explained, 'I can't let you come down yet, but you can have a look from the side.'

Lomond started towards the tent. 'Let's see what we've got.'

Moira stayed down in the hole in full protective gear. She pulled her hood back, then did something that took Lomond, Ross, and Willie by surprise.

She smiled.

'Been a while since we caught an old one,' she said.

The three men stood side by side at the edge of the hole, assessing the scene. There wasn't much to make of it. At first glance anyway.

A clear plastic bag with sealed ends lay partially covered by mud and dirt and rocks, revealing a human skeleton inside. Moira had opened the bag at the top, slicing carefully down the centre to examine the bones.

But tangled among the bones and around the skull were what looked like leather straps.

Lomond crouched down for a closer look. 'Are we talking a John or Jane Doe?'

'Judging by pelvic bone structure, mastoid processes–' She could immediately tell that she had lost Lomond and the others. She gestured to a point behind her ear lobe. 'It's a bony projection at the base of the temporal bones on each side of the skull. Females have very small to small-sized mastoids. Males' are much larger.'

Lomond said, 'Once the press gets wind of this, there's going to be a lot of very worried families with missing relatives from the time period. I need an identity – with certainty – as soon as possible.'

Moira gestured at her surroundings. 'There's barely room for just me and the skeleton down here, John. Can you maybe give me more than half an hour to make a positive ID on decades' old remains?'

There it is, thought Lomond. The Moira Dreich that he knew and loved.

Though he couldn't help but notice a small bulge under her blue medical glove. It was on her ring finger.

Moira, glanced down quickly at her hand, then realised what had made Lomond smile. She smiled back.

Unseen by the others, Lomond mouthed, 'Congrats,' then winked at her.

Ross, always eager to sound professional and impress Lomond, asked, 'Are there any environmental factors that could have been in play?'

Moira paused, lips pursed. She turned to both Willie and Lomond with a confused glare before answering. 'Well, I'm ruling out accidental drowning in the river followed by self-burial, if that's what you're asking.'

Lomond and Willie shared a wry smirk with each other. Moira Dreich was cracking jokes at discovery scenes now?

Ross shrugged. 'I don't know. I'm just thinking out loud.'

'Thinking,' repeated Moira. 'Really? Is that what that was?'

'I was thinking about anthropological analysis. You know, age and ancestry can help narrow down potential matches with missing persons.'

Willie suggested, 'I'm pretty sure that's occurred to Moira, DS McNair.'

Lomond said, 'Did you Google that on the way over or something?'

Ross couldn't bring himself to admit it had been something he had heard on *Silent Witness* on the BBC a few weeks earlier, and had filed it away in his brain in case it could prove useful sometime.

Moira said, 'For how long she'd been buried, she's in decent condition. I'm confident we'll be able to identify her.'

'How long has she been in the ground?' asked Lomond.

'If pushed to answer, I would say anywhere between fifteen and twenty years. But in remains this old, until I've done lab work, there's a good plus or minus of five years either side of that.'

Ross asked, 'Will it help that the body's been in a bag?'

'It won't hurt,' Moira replied. 'Moisture accelerates decomposition, the skeleton has been protected from physical damage having been secured underground...'

Secured, Lomond and Willie thought. That was one way of putting it.

Moira went on, 'I don't see any evidence of chemicals for the purposes of preservation, though it was an airtight seal on the bag.'

'Why would someone do that?' asked Willie. 'Instead of just wrapping it up loose?'

'Masking smell when you're burying someone so deep isn't a factor. I don't know.' Moira deferred to Lomond.

He said, 'That's a question mark for me. You're burying a body deep under the ground. What is it, seven feet down there you reckon, Moira?'

She had a look around. 'About that.'

'That can't have been done by hand, surely. It would take several hours to dig that far down with a shovel.' Lomond did a quick three-sixty of the area. They were directly across the river from the Riverside Museum – previously known as the Transport Museum, rehoused from its old location in the Kelvin Hall – and residential housing was just a stone's throw away behind them.

Ross, who had been tapping away and pinch-zooming on

his phone screen, showed Lomond what he had been doing. 'This is Google maps from two thousand and eight. It's a pretty different proposition.'

Lomond sucked in air. 'Aye, not half.' He handed the phone to Willie.

The patch of scrubland where the construction site had taken over had previously been fenced off and completely overgrown.

Ross said, 'It's not like those houses over there are tall. And look at how many more trees there used to be here. Now change the date to just four years later.'

Willie stared at the phone like he'd been handed alien technology. 'How do I do that?'

Ross rolled his eyes and snatched the phone back. 'Look,' he said, and with a few taps on the screen showed the change of scene.

Gone was the tall silver fence, overgrown scrub, and dense trees.

Ross continued, 'From the old walkway you couldn't even see the north side of the river. Someone could have plugged away at digging a hole in advance without anyone noticing. This grave would have been right in the middle of these trees here and behind the fence blocking off access to the riverside. Jump ahead to twenty fourteen, and all that scrub's gone to build the riverside walkway. Ten years ago, the killer could never have got away with burying her here. This whole area would have been wide open.' Ross pointed behind them. 'Govan Cross is barely thirty seconds walk away over there. Govan and Linthouse Parish is right there. You couldnae be digging a grave here back then.'

Ross had a habit of speaking looser when around both Willie and Lomond together – an unconscious attempt to loosen up his speech patterns, to sound more like one of the guys.

Lomond nodded, impressed at how quickly Ross had put it together. 'So she must have been buried more than ten years ago.'

'That makes sense,' Willie agreed.

'How old was she, do you think?' asked Lomond. 'At the end.'

Moira bobbed her head from side to side. 'Given the degree of fusion and ossification of bones, bone histology, the epiphyseal union...' she crouched down to indicate the area around the thigh bone, 'that's the rounded ends of bones. You can tell from the fusion of the epiphyses with the diaphysis – that's the shaft of the bone – which occurs during late teenage years, early adulthood, that we're talking over eighteen. My visual assessment of the fusion, I would say she was closer to twenty, twenty-five. There's little degenerative changes in joints to indicate advanced aging that would associate with someone over the age of forty.'

'I'm more interested in that,' said Lomond, pointing to the leather straps around the skull.'

'Some kind of bondage thing?' Willie speculated.

'Maybe some sex game gone wrong?' Ross offered. 'What would have been a secluded spot here years back might have been somewhere for a pro to work. Maybe got into someone's car.'

'This isn't that,' said Lomond, still looking at the bones. 'This was too prepared. Too studied. The hole had to have been dug. And what about that bag, Moira? You don't get them wandering down your local B&Q.'

'No,' she agreed. 'These are medical grade sacks. Not body

bags per se. This one's been folded over along the sides for a better fit.'

'Could it be traceable?'

She shook her head. 'I mean, if this had been last week it would have helped narrow things down. I might be able to get you a manufacturer, but in the time frame you're working with, you'll never be able to track down a buyer.'

Willie crouched down next to Lomond. 'What even *is* that thing?'

Ross crouched down beside Willie. 'It's a bridle.'

The pair turned and stared at him.

'You know,' said Ross. 'Like for a horse. It goes around the head and connects to the reins. It's an important part of riding. It's how a rider communicates with the horse.'

'How d'you know all this Frankie Dettori?' asked Willie.

'Isla used to ride before we had Lachlann. She took me to the stables a couple of times.' Realising that this wasn't quite appeasing their curiosity, he shrugged. 'I remember things.'

Lomond sighed. 'Shite.'

'Why "shite"?' Willie asked.

'For one thing, the bag shows preparation. It demonstrates premeditation at least. Even if it was a crime of passion, there was no panic. For someone's first time, they want to clean the scene and get as far away as possible, as quickly as possible. If anything, this guy hung around.' He thought further, taking his time. 'I'll bet they drew it out. I'm saying "they", but it's almost certainly a "he". It's specific. I mean, very specific. How many victims have you ever found with a horse's...what was it again, Ross? Bridle?'

'Aye,' Ross replied.

'Whoever did this had a real plan in mind. The bridle. The bag. Even the burial.'

'What do you mean?' asked Willie.

'Why bother with any of it? Unless the act had meaning. They could have just buried the body without a bag. They didn't even need to bury it. Why bury it? A body hidden in scrubland next to the river could have gone unnoticed for weeks, even months. You throw in the fact that the bag was airtight...' He trailed off, still assembling his conclusion.

Moira said, 'Do you think the killer wanted to preserve the body?'

'We're not talking embalming here, or formaldehyde. But I think there was a degree of preservation going on here. Again, an act that must have had meaning. Why seal a body bag you're about to bury in a tonne of dirt and never going to see again?'

Willie asked, 'What are the teeth looking like, Moira?'

She nodded cautiously. 'I can work with them. Whether they get you a match on anyone is another matter.'

Lomond put his hand out to apologise for interrupting. 'Moira, can I step down for a sec?'

She pointed at his feet. 'Shoe covers, please. And gloves.'

Lomond slid some plastic shoe covers on and plastic gloves, then carefully lowered himself down with Moira's helping hand.

She went on, 'My suggestion is that without a dental records match, your best bet of identifying the victim is for us to give you a spectrum of estimates. With lab work I can get you results on skeletal development, dental development, and a decent histological analysis. Long bone measurements, pelvic dimensions, statistical methods can all help with stature estimation to give you height. With those factors together, I think you could find someone through missing persons records of the period.'

While Moira went on about the minutiae of the lab work

she could perform, using an array of the latest technology that cost millions of pounds to buy, Lomond took out an old biro from his jacket pocket and looped it through one of the leather straps. He'd caught something glinting in the sunlight that had broken through the patchy clouds above. Shifting the strap aside, he could now see a necklace still looped around the victim's neck.

He reached down towards the pendant, a silver heart. Then he opened it.

Moira broke off as she noticed what Lomond was doing. She snapped, 'Gently, John.'

He didn't flinch. He already had the answer he was looking for. He kept the biro looped around the locket chain, holding up the opened heart pendant for Moira to see.

'What have you got?' asked Willie.

Inside the pendant was a picture of a woman in her sixties.

'The identity of the victim,' Lomond replied.

'How can you be sure?' Ross asked.

Lomond unhooked the clasp on the locket, then showed it to the men. 'Because about twenty years ago I sat in that woman's living room and promised I would find her daughter. This wasn't exactly the way I intended to find her.'

CHAPTER FOUR

Detective Constable Donna Higgins was in the bullpen of the Major Investigations office, sitting across from DC Jason Yang and DC Pardeep Varma. All three of them were on their computers, combing through missing persons records.

On the mezzanine above, staring out of her window overlooking the office, was Detective Superintendent Linda Boyle. She knocked heavily on the window: a police officer's knock. Hard and insistent.

Donna, Jason, and Pardeep all looked quickly up at her in unison.

Linda pointed aggressively at something, but from such a distance away it was unclear what.

Donna held her hands out to indicate that she was clueless.

Linda shook her head with a roll of the eyes, then marched towards her door. Hands on hips, like an angry neighbour yelling at someone to get off their lawn, she called out, 'Stop faffing about!'

The three constables looked at one another in confusion.

Linda elaborated, 'I've been watching you lot reading

through files, taking your time. If it fits with the dates that John's given you, lob it into the pile of "maybes". And Donna, get up here.'

Out of earshot, Pardeep winced on Donna's behalf. 'Good luck with that,' he said. 'She's obviously short of a coffee or two this morning.'

Donna stood up, buttoning her suit jacket. 'Her department's just caught a ten-to-twenty-year-old cold case. We're lucky she's not set the building on fire yet.'

Jason checked his watch – a bulky number with about fifty separate data fields on the face, and looked like it might have air traffic navigation capability. 'It's not even lunchtime, Donna. Give her a chance.'

Donna felt her stomach churn on her way up the stairs. She had a feeling about what was coming her way. It had been in the post for at least the last month. But Linda had been letting her stew on it.

'Shut the door,' said Linda, finishing off typing something on her phone.

She sounded so grave, for a moment Donna thought she might be getting fired.

Donna hesitated behind the chair across from Linda, unsure whether to go straight to sitting, or wait to be invited to do so.

She decided to stand, which was wise.

The irritation with which Linda tossed her phone down on her desk made it obvious she was in no mood for pleasantries.

'It's time to decide who you're going to be, Donna,' said Linda.

Donna turned her head slightly. 'I don't understand.'

Linda went on, 'You took part in a drug deal in order to

track down your dad, then DCI Lomond caught you about to open a sealed MAPPA file in the records room.'

Donna replied, 'I was trying to find the location of a missing child, ma'am. And if I hadn't have tracked down my dad we would never have found out about–'

'You broke the law. Which is sort of the opposite of what we do around here. If John hadn't lied to a Professional Standards committee you would have been out on your ear.'

'I never asked for him to–'

'I know you didn't ask him to lie, Donna. But John Lomond is John Lomond, and he was never going to risk one of his own over a misplaced desire to break a case.' Linda sighed, transitioning to the encouraging part of their conversation. 'I don't know if you've looked around here lately, but there are good police, and there are bad police. You and John are better than good. And I nearly lost the pair of you. Do you know who replaces you if you two go out on some flyer like that again without telling me first?' She lowered her voice conspiratorially. 'I get knobheads like DCI Peter Duffy. Or worse yet, we might even get handed DCI Ruth Telford. But the day she takes John's place in front of that whiteboard will also be the day that either hell freezes over, or I drop dead from the massive coronary that I'm probably overdue.'

'What would you like me to do, ma'am?' asked Donna earnestly. 'I didn't come here to muck around. I want to work.'

'I don't want your past catching up with you, and costing you your future.' Linda waited a beat. 'I read the report about what your dad did. To your mum.'

Donna straightened her back at the mere mention of it.

Even for someone of Linda Boyle's experience the report had been a tough read. DC Higgins' dad had been on a three-day coke bender when he chained Donna's mum to a radiator.

One of the old-style ones with bars. After he'd beaten Donna almost to unconsciousness, she had been left bleeding on the floor, helpless as he beat her mum half to death in front of her.

She was barely ten years old at the time.

Donna said, 'There's a lot that my dad did that never made it into any report.'

'I don't doubt it, Donna. My dad beat the shit out of me, as did my first husband. I've been there. And I'm not telling you that because I'm trying to beat you at Domestic Violence Top Trumps or something. I'm telling you because I get it. I see a lot of me in you. I'll leave it up to you whether you think that's a good thing. But I don't want these pricks on Professional Standards tripping you up. They don't like women like us, Donna. It doesn't matter around here if a guy's a bit lippy. It might even be a benefit. But for a woman, the crowd at Mordor don't like it when you give a little bit back. If we want to make it, we need to be twice as good as the guy across the desk. That's just a fact.'

'Ma'am, this is encouraging and all that,' said Donna, 'but I've got a thousand missing persons files that you want me to get through by lunchtime with the boys.'

'You want me to cut to the chase?' asked Linda. 'It's hard enough to progress around here. Don't give them easy wins by breaking the law. And don't risk my best officers' careers in the process. Got it?'

'Yes, ma'am,' Donna replied, nodding appreciatively,

'Right,' Linda said, returning to her computer screen. 'Sod off back to work.'

Once Donna got to the door, Linda called her back. 'And Donna...if you tell anyone about my dad and ex-husband...' She trailed off. She didn't even have to mention the repercussions.

Donna nodded. 'Of course, ma'am.'

Before Donna could get back to her desk, DCI Lomond returned with Willie and Ross in tow.

CHAPTER FIVE

LOMOND'S WALK was the purposeful kind that let the others know he meant business. Marching to the whiteboard as if he had information in his head he wanted to get down before it was forgotten.

With a single word, he brought the room to attention.

'Right,' he declared, then scrawled a name in capital letters on the whiteboard.

"LIANNE GRIBBIN"

Ross and Willie joined Donna, Pardeep, and Jason by their desks.

Lomond turned to face his team. 'We've got a preliminary ID on the body. We need to wait for forensics, of course, but...' He trailed off, staring at the thin carpet. He shook his head slowly.

Donna looked at Ross. Ross looked at Willie. No one wanted to be the one to interrupt whatever was going on inside Lomond's head.

He looked up again. 'There's a piece of jewellery around

the deceased's neck. An item that was listed for identification purposes in the missing person case of Lianne Gribbin.' He gave Willie the nod.

Willie handed each of the team a copy of the same file.

Lomond said, 'As you can see from the date, the case goes back twenty years. Lianne was twenty-three at the time of her disappearance. She'd been working as a prostitute for a year, flying solo mostly–'

Pardeep let out a puff. He knew from his experience working the city centre beat as a constable how risky it was for someone new on the streets to operate in such a way. Most of the women he'd encountered on the job worked in a tight-knit circle, staying in contact regularly, picking up clients within sight of the other women. It at least meant that they could keep tabs on familiar cars. Most of the woman had regulars. Anyone new instantly drew suspicion.

Lomond went on, 'And judging by Pardeep's reaction, he knows only too well the risks involved with that. Lianne didn't have any experience or information on who to stay away from. Who was rough, who was to be avoided. Eventually she fell in with a crowd who worked near Tradeston. They kept tabs on each other. One night, Lianne didn't show up, and that was it. It was as if she'd disappeared off the face of the earth. None of her closest associates or friends had seen her getting into any vehicles. The only eyewitness statements we could get about someone matching her description on the night of her disappearance were either contradictory or inconclusive.'

'Were there ever any suspects?' Ross asked.

Lomond nodded. 'There was a boyfriend, Thomas Rafferty. A right piece of work. But there was never any evidence. Forensics trawled through his flat. Nothing. His car.

Nothing. No evidence of a struggle. No blood. No sudden purchases of bleach or cleaning products in the middle of the night. Like a lot of young women, Lianne Gribbin disappeared and that was that. She wasn't even a statistic. She was less than that. She was simply forgotten about. Except for her mum.' Lomond paused. The memory of the woman seemingly striking a chord deep within him. 'She never stopped looking.'

Jason asked, 'What were you back then, sir? Detective constable?'

Willie folded his arms and smiled sardonically, like a pal of someone's dad who was about to make fun of what Jason had said. He nodded in Lomond's direction. 'How old do you think he *is*, son?'

Jason's cheeks flushed at the thought of embarrassing Lomond in front of the others.

Lomond pursed his lips, knowing Jason hadn't meant anything by it. 'Detective Sergeant, Jase.'

Ross asked, 'What happened with the enquiry?'

'This was back in Strathclyde Police days,' Lomond explained. 'At the time it was just another missing person case. No one gave it much thought, to be honest. Due to her profession, the lack of connection to the other working girls in the area, there wasn't much for us to go on. Every year, nine thousand people are reported missing in this country. Within twenty-four hours, seventy-seven per cent of adults and eighty-one per cent of children are found. Common reasons for going missing?' He looked up expectedly at the team.

Donna answered first. 'For adults, mental health issues or relationship breakdowns. For children, it's conflict or neglect at home.'

'Correct,' said Lomond, giving away no clue of his pleasure

at the textbook answer. 'What makes missing persons harder when that person works as a prostitute?'

Pardeep answered, 'You're dealing with people who aren't always missed. There's a transient nature to the job. A lot of drugs are involved. When money's earned, that can mean someone goes off the scene for weeks at a time.'

'Lianne did have drug issues,' Lomond said. 'Without Lianne's mum, her disappearance might never have gone reported. It was my job to go around the streets with a photo of Lianne and find out if anyone on the street had any information. Willie and I worked it.'

'Yeah,' Willie said. 'Not a great look from the outside. Two police officers wandering around Tradeston at night approaching prostitutes.'

Donna remarked, 'From what I hear, you wouldn't have been the only officers out there at night.'

An uncomfortable silence followed.

The MIT constables looked at each other nervously.

Rumours of police officers using prostitutes had broken in the tabloids around the same time as Lianne's disappearance. The scandal was only ever spoken about in hushed tones, whispered about across desks, shared in patrol cars, as rumours of who had been involved spread like wildfire.

What Donna hadn't realised was that for older officers like Lomond and Willie, there had been a widespread *omertà* on the topic. It was common knowledge which officers had used prostitutes. Many of whom abused their positions of authority to demand free sex from the women who were too scared to be collared for a section forty-six – prostitution – to ever report any of the incidents. Or in some cases, assaults.

The offending officers mostly had reputations that

preceded them, and the worst had mostly been spirited quietly out of the force many years ago. But Lomond and Willie knew of a few who had survived the rumour mill, and even ascended to the heights of Dalmarnock, or even to the Police Scotland executive team at Tulliallan.

Donna panicked at the off-the-cuff remark she had casually thrown out, which, to Lomond and Willie, had gone over like a pregnant pole vaulter.

Eager to move on, and after giving Donna a withering look, Lomond said, 'No one knew anything. The only information linked to a white saloon of unknown origin. No registration plate. It proved impossible to follow up. One of the women handed over their Beware Book for us to check, but we didn't find any suspicious matches.'

'Beware Book?' Jason said.

Lomond motioned. 'Pardeep, you want to tell him?'

Pardeep told Jason, 'A Beware Book is something that goes around the women, detailing any men to be wary of, or just stay away from – refuse to do business with. There's a lot of scary, violent men out there who use prostitutes to deal with their... proclivities is the charitable way of putting it.'

Willie elaborated, 'Men who are into beating up women, strangling them, or worse.'

Lomond nodded. 'The Beware Book made for grim reading. Sexual assault and rape were commonplace. There was hardly a woman who had written in the book who hadn't experienced it. The sad truth is, there are plenty of sexually violent dangerous men out there. Murderers in waiting, frankly. There's so many of them, we don't have any way of stopping them until it's too late. That's just the reality. And the men know it too.'

For detective constables like Donna and Jason, with relatively little experience of such realities, it made for sobering listening. They had become detectives in order to do good, to protect the innocent, and bring criminals – dangerous people – to justice. Now Lomond was telling them that there was a vast underbelly of such people operating in Glasgow with impunity.

CHAPTER SIX

LOMOND CONTINUED, 'Making a case against these men is almost impossible. Even if you could get one to trial, the nature of the profession and the women involved makes them pretty easy targets for ambitious defence lawyers with win records to protect. Suffice to say, the investigation slowed up after the first few weeks. Then we were thrown another three to work on. Those were all resolved, but Lianne Gribbin was quickly forgotten about. I must admit, even by myself. Until today.'

Pardeep wagged a pen as he consulted the case file, then raised his hand. 'Sir, it says here that Detective Superintendent Boyle was SIO. Is that right?'

Lomond paused, glancing up towards her office. 'She was Detective Inspector at the time. In Strathclyde Police days a missing prostitute never got much higher than a DI. It's horrible to admit out loud, but it was just routine. But that was then. This is now. When Lianne disappeared, our focus was on a certain sort of guy. But what was uncovered by the bridge this morning wasn't the work of some regular john wrapped up in an impulsive moment of violence. I doubt it happened because Lianne refused to do something. I'll bet that by the time she was in close quarters with her killer, there's not a thing she could have done to stop it. The digging of the grave, the preparation for it, the planning, the logistics, the choosing of the site, all indicate premeditation of a worrying kind. This killer has deeper purpose, I think. Certainly not someone out of control in the sense that they don't know what they're doing.'

Willie handed out the forensics photos taken so far.

Lomond took one and pinned it to the board. It showed Lianne's skeleton, and the horse's bridle installed around her skull.

The team squinted at the photos.

'What is that thing?' asked Pardeep.

'Some S&M bit of kit?' Donna wondered.

'It's a horse bridle,' Ross answered. 'It's what connects the reins to the horse's head for the rider to communicate with it.'

Lomond pointed at the photo on the board. 'Is that evidence of a killer looking to demonstrate control? Acting out some fantasy of coercion?'

'Could be a deeper symbology or iconography,' Jason suggested.

Lomond lifted his head, eager to hear the reasoning. 'Like what?'

'Horses have played an important role in mythology through the centuries,' said Jason. 'There could be any number of interpretations that are meaningful to the killer. For violent men who just enjoy violent sex, or even just violence itself, acting out impulses is reward enough. They don't need props.'

Lomond nodded slowly. He knew that out of the team, Jason would be the one with the nuanced knowledge to suggest such a thing. 'I agree,' Lomond said. 'Like a good film director, killers like this one don't leave things visible or prominent by accident.'

Jason said, 'Maybe the bridle could offer a way forward for the enquiry. I mean, you didn't have a body back then, and you obviously didn't have the bridle. If we're lucky, and the meaning behind the device is as we suspect, it might be something exotic. We might get lucky. I can't imagine there was much of anything in the way of productions in Lianne's disappearance.'

Productions was police talk for items relating to a crime scene.

Lomond replied, 'There *was* no crime scene. Lianne lived in a hostel at the time. There was nothing in her room to indicate a crime.' He picked up the original case file. 'This is all we've got to go on, and whatever else Moira finds us from the body. But I wouldn't get your hopes up.'

Willie said, 'Devil's advocate, but what if it's not Lianne...'

Lomond admitted, 'It's a leap based on one piece of jewellery. I get that. But until we get an identity, the fact is that Lianne Gribbin's pendant has been found on human remains. I'd say that warrants investigation, no matter the identity of the victim.'

Turning his palms up, Jason asked, 'How do we investigate this, boss? An enquiry like this, we can't rely on any of the usual methodology.'

'I'm glad someone's mentioned that,' said Lomond. 'Because actually we investigate it the same way we do any other murder. And no matter what happens here, I want you all to remember a little something. I've worked a few cases like this. And whenever human remains are found, it's bad for a lot of people, of course. Not least the family of the victim. It's also bad for us because it means that a previous investigation failed.

Either an unresolved murder enquiry, or a missing person – like Lianne Gribbin – who was never found. But the process of how we correct that failure is the same as always. Track down the key suspects. Like Thomas Rafferty.' Lomond sought out Pardeep and Jason. 'You two. Get me an address for him.'

The two men rose gingerly.

'Anywhere we should try first, boss?' asked Pardeep.

Lomond replied, 'Check under the CPO.'

It stood for Community Payback Order – the system that replaced probation. CPO imposed unpaid work or supervision on offenders once released from jail.

Lomond explained, 'Apparently he was inside recently.'

Jason asked, 'What was he in for?'

'I don't know yet.'

Donna said, 'And there was nothing to pin Lianne's disappearance on Rafferty?'

Willie drummed his fingers on the desk he'd been leaning on. 'We tried. But there was never anything conclusive. Looks like we might have missed something.'

Lomond assured the team, 'I always liked Rafferty for this. But that scene today...the Thomas Rafferty I spoke to all those years ago couldn't manage something like that. He was a brutal bastard, but let's just say his lift didn't exactly go to the top floor, if you know what I mean.' Lomond held up a warning finger. 'Do not make the mistake of approaching this any differently than any other murder enquiry. You hear me? Talk to key witnesses again. And yes, people forget after twenty years, but there's nothing we can do about that. Strathclyde Police sat on its hands when Lianne Gribbin went missing. Let's at least give her mother the justice she deserves. We're doing this properly...' He trailed off, noticing a number of junior constables entering the Major Investigations office at the back, all pushing trolleys loaded with cardboard boxes. 'That's why I've asked for the files of every missing woman in the last thirty years, in case there are other Lianne Gribbins out there.'

The team looked as one at the intimidating sight of dozens of boxes all rammed with files, being offloaded in the bullpen – all anyone could think about was the scale of the task in front of them, and how little sleep anyone would be getting for a while.

Lomond continued, 'I've also ordered a complete excavation of the bridge construction site. If Lianne Gribbin wasn't the first – or last – and the killer found a place they could trust, who knows what else – or who else – is under the concrete that's already been laid–'

From Detective Superintendent Linda Boyle's office on the mezzanine overlooking the bullpen, there was a piercing howl of Lomond's first name. The sort of shriek one would expect if Lomond had walked out in front of traffic without realising it. There was life-and-death urgency to it. 'JOHN!'

Lomond turned to Willie, 'Well, we knew this would happen, eh.'

Willie shrugged nonchalantly.

A further bellow rang out from Linda. 'Get up here now!'

CHAPTER SEVEN

'OH SHIT,' Lomond puffed as he went up the stairs, dreading what he was about to get. Before he was in the room he could already hear the Grand Arsehole himself – Chief Superintendent Alasdair Reekie – on a conference call with DSU Linda Boyle.

Reekie's voice was muffled by the closed door, but Lomond could make out Linda's pleas. 'I know, Alasdair, I know...that's exactly what I'm about to tell him...'

Lomond opened the door. 'Linda.' He spoke up a little. 'Sir.'

While Reekie charged into a tirade, Linda hit the mute button on her phone.

She said, 'He's angrier than a mosquito in a mannequin factory, John. You've no idea the arse ache I've had to put up with because of you.'

'What have I done?' asked Lomond, even though he already suspected.

Various snippets of Reekie's tirade were still audible underneath their conversation. Lomond managed to make out:

'...any idea how much money has been invested in that bridge?'

And:

'...this will set back construction by months...'

Linda released the mute button, then motioned for Lomond to get involved.

He stepped closer to the desk, but Reekie was still ranting.

'Do you *know* what's happened?' Reekie demanded.

'Not entirely, sir,' Lomond replied.

'I've had the project manager for the bridge on the phone wanting to know under whose authority can the construction site be shut down, and an excavation of the grounds be ordered. I was confused, John. Because only I have the authority in this area to grant such a request. And the only request I've made this morning is for Linda to throw you out of the nearest window.'

Lomond tried to interject. 'Sir, I know you're angry–'

'That's not the only call I've had, by the way. I've had – amongst others – the Lord Provost, and leader of the City Council. Two people with considerably more authority than John Lomond.'

'I have reason to believe there are more bodies in that area. This killer got away with it this long. When killers get away with it, they stick to the same plan.'

'I agree,' said Linda tentatively, 'but that points to someone using the same method but at a different site, John. The last thing a killer wants is to draw attention to where he's put the first body.'

Lomond countered, 'If Lianne Gribbin was indeed the first.'

Reekie fired back, 'You're talking like it was the Burma railway over there. You've got one body!'

Lomond couldn't argue with that.

Reekie went on, 'And clearly you haven't considered the political ramifications of excavating the site. That sort of thing can't be hidden from the press. Do you think all those construction workers who read the *Glasgow Express* every day aren't going to call up the Colin Mowatts of this world and tell him they've been sent home indefinitely, and their diggers are now being used to break up the ground they've just put down nearby?'

Linda added, 'That's when the press are going to ask what we think is under there. Suddenly we've turned twenty-year-old remains into news of a potential serial killer on the loose.'

Lomond raised his eyebrows. 'I wouldn't be too quick to rule that out. And this isn't the first time I've been asked to bury bad news.'

Linda pursed her lips tightly and shook her head urgently. But it was too late.

Reekie replied, 'I suppose you think that little dig is enough to get what you want, John.'

'It crossed my mind, sir.'

Linda shut her eyes, then backed away from the phone with a shrug, as if to say, *I've tried to protect you, but now you're on your own.*

Reekie said, 'You've got some nerve, John. There's a detective constable down there at Major Investigations who should have been brought up on charges of tampering with evidence. And you covered up for her. She should be in cuffs, that one.'

'Well, as long as we're discussing charges, sir, it wasn't me who killed the Professional Standards proceedings against Donna Higgins. It was Assistant Chief Constable Niven, when new evidence came to light.'

'Yeah, thanks to me,' was Reekie's caustic response.

'And as myself and Donna were fully exonerated, we're very grateful that justice was served.'

'Let's cut the crap, John. You got your ex, DCI Ruth Telford, to lean on Niven. God knows what she had on him after all those boozy nights out over curries when they worked together in Aberdeen. Him and his bloody wandering hands after he'd had a couple of lagers, the lightweight. It didn't take long for Niven to lean on me. Unlike you, I understand and respect hierarchy. So I did what I was told. I covered for you. As well as Donna, god help me.'

Lomond replied, 'You nearly cost us a chance at catching a child killer. I wasn't the one who messed up an enquiry–'

Linda had heard enough. 'John!'

The shout was loud enough to pierce the closed window, and for everyone downstairs to look up.

Calmer now, Linda said, 'We're all senior colleagues here, John, but watch it.'

Reekie said, 'We did *quid pro quo* last time, John. That's over now. This excavation is never going to happen. The bridge isn't even built yet. A symbol of connecting two sides of the city, of bringing people together. And you want to insinuate that it is in fact the location of a mass grave! Do you know how much money's been invested in this bridge? And what that money's going to do for the city? You don't get to dismantle that.'

Lomond replied, 'Politics isn't my concern. Public relations isn't my concern. But catching a killer is. Lianne may or may not have been the killer's first, but I'd be amazed if she was his last. Not when they so clearly got away with it for so long. That need, that drive to kill, doesn't just go away when you've done it once. Not for this guy. Not from what I saw this morning. The bridle was symbolic. Important. Jason could see it too.'

'Bridle?' said Reekie. 'What are you talking about?'

Linda, rather reluctantly, said, 'There was a horse's bridle around the skull. As if the victim had been made to wear it at time of death.'

'She was a hooker, wasn't she? It will have been some sick sex thing.'

Perfect, Lomond thought, eyebrows thrown up at the predictable dismissal of the bridle's importance. It was easier for Reekie to assume that Lianne's demise had come about because of a client's strange fetish. The alternative – that a killer had been operating with greater purpose than a crime of passion or violent simplicity – wasn't something Reekie was ready to entertain.

Trying to get back to the actual investigation, Linda said, 'Killer's kinks aside, first of all, the press are going to get wind of this with or without an excavation of the site. So John, you need to get over to Lianne Gribbin's family with an FLO and tell her what's coming. It's bad enough we never found her daughter. Let's not bungle the communication as well.'

Lomond, hands on hips now, said, 'I don't want a family liaison officer there. I don't need it, and neither does Brenda.'

'Who's Brenda?' asked Reekie, then remembered. 'Oh, the mum. Right.'

Lomond said, 'I want one of my own in there with me.'

'Who?'

'Donna.'

'No chance,' said Reekie. 'I want her benched.'

'You can't do that, Alasdair,' Lomond insisted. 'She was cleared.'

'I don't care. I want her benched on this one, then quietly moved on.'

Linda gestured for him to let it go. 'That's fine, sir,' she answered, while shaking her head at Lomond.

'Right, I've got a queue outside my door,' Reekie complained. 'Let me know when you know anything. And if you can prioritise any methods that don't involve a massive public relations disaster, that would be appreciated.'

Before Linda could respond, Reekie hung up.

The line had barely gone dead when Lomond said, 'Like hell I'm benching Donna...'

'I know,' Linda said.

'She was getting FLO experience at Mill Street before she came here. It makes sense.'

Linda gestured for him to calm down. 'I *know*, John. But it's going to make life easier for us both now that Reekie's finished the call getting at least one thing that he wants.'

'Sometimes I forget there's a reason you're up here and I'm down there.'

She grinned. 'There are a *lot* of reasons why that's the case. But you'd better have a plan, John. You're the one fucking this donkey. I'm just the one left holding the tail. What's next?'

'The boyfriend,' said Lomond. 'Thomas Rafferty.'

Linda puffed. 'That's a name I was happier forgetting. You really think he was capable of planning the burial? And all this weird horse stuff?'

'No,' said Lomond. 'But he knew more than he was letting on back then...' He craned his neck to look out the window.

Jason was holding up piece of paper and giving a thumbs up.

Lomond said distantly, heading towards the door. 'Maybe he still is.'

Linda sat back down behind her desk. 'Oh, bye then...'

Once downstairs, Pardeep informed Lomond, 'We've got an address on Rafferty. He was inside, right enough.'

Unable to hide the glint in his eye, Jason said, 'Guess what he was in for.'

'What?' said Lomond.

Pardeep answered as if the entire case had been solved. 'Attempted abduction and attempted sexual assault.'

Everyone else who heard it stopped in their tracks.

Lomond said, 'Get on him. Pronto. Good work, boys.' Then he turned to Donna, who was rummaging through boxes of old missing person files. 'Donna, get your jacket.'

Ross had been hovering in such a way that Lomond knew he had something he wanted to talk to him about. And Lomond didn't want any part of it.

Ross began, 'I know this isn't a good time...'

Lomond had to fight not to roll his eyes. 'Ross, I swear sometimes if you fell you'd miss the ground.'

Ross squinted, not fully understanding the insult. 'I wasn't sure if I'd catch you later. It's just, Isla's pal Catriona mentioned that you and her were going out, and I wanted to let you know...'

Willie looked on in amusement as Ross attempted a light, slow motion punch on Lomond's shoulder, as if they were best buds.

Ross concluded, 'I think that's a really good thing.'

Willie laughed. 'You couldn't time a fart in a curry house, son.'

Lomond stared back. 'I cancelled. Like most of your little attempts at camaraderie, it's not a good time, Ross.'

Hovering by her desk, Donna added, 'I think you should do it, boss.'

To Lomond's dismay, even Willie joined in. 'Aye, John.

The time's never right. You don't wait for your life to settle down. Your life settles down when you find somebody.'

Lomond whipped around, as if looking for an audience that wasn't there. 'I'm sorry, has this police station turned into the set of Eastenders, or something?' Noticing Pardeep and Jason straggling by their desks, Lomond called out, 'You two...' He thumbed to the side. 'Get tae.' He turned to Willie and Ross. 'This wasn't taken seriously back then. We're going to correct that now. We need to go back over everything like it's day one. That means we turn Lianne's life from twenty years ago inside out. Starting with...' He waited for an answer.

Willie trusted Ross to get it.

'Where she was living,' Ross said.

Lomond then pointed to Donna. 'And you, Lorraine bloody Kelly. Come with me.'

Donna quickly grabbed her jacket, then rushed to catch up. 'Where are we going?'

Lomond stormed ahead. 'To see Lianne Gribbin's mum.' He paused to clap his hands. 'It's time to get our game faces on, ladies and gents. Let's go...'

CHAPTER EIGHT

LOMOND AND DONNA came off the M8 westbound at Hillington Interchange next to Braehead, then quickly found themselves within the grey labyrinth of the Afton housing estate.

An endless series of speed bumps kept them under twenty miles an hour, giving them time to take in the winding streets made up of detached and semi-detached grey houses, and almost identical gardens. The same vertical Venetian blinds hung in seemingly every living room window.

Driving towards Brenda Gribbin's house, Lomond was reminded of a time he had walked the same route he used to take to primary school. It took him a moment to realise why everything seemed so small—he had been a few feet shorter the last time he was there. Though Lomond hadn't changed much in size since his last visit to the estate, he felt the same sense of nostalgic disorientation as he had when retracing his childhood steps.

'Seems nice,' Donna offered.

'I suppose.' Lomond's eyes were drawn to kids' toys left in

front gardens. Basketball nets attached to garages. An image of family life he'd always assumed would one day be his own. The idea of his ever having somewhere with his own garden seemed unlikely to him now. The way his life had turned out, living in flats seemed more practical. He had no interest in gardening, and no practical need for somewhere for a child to run around.

When they reached Brenda Gribbin's street, it all came flooding back to him.

Lomond stopped outside the house. By quite a margin, it had the neatest front garden on the street – probably the whole estate. As if each blade of grass had been individually trimmed. The front door looked recently painted. Even from the street, the house inside looked immaculate. Lace curtains hung in perfect symmetry in the window. There was nothing on the living room couches but a few scatter cushions. No clutter, no mess. It looked like someone had prepared for visitors, but Lomond could have appeared without warning on any day of the year and found the place in the same condition.

In any case, Brenda Gribbin had been given no indication the police were coming.

It was a far cry from the house he'd entered twenty years ago. Such a stark contrast, in fact, Lomond double-checked they had the right address.

Then he saw Brenda rising from an armchair, as she noticed the silver Mondeo idling in front of the house. Lomond recognised her instantly – despite the usual signs of aging you would expect from someone you hadn't seen in twenty years. She was wearing a bright floral dress that went down to the ankle. The majority of her wardrobe consisted of such dresses, all bought in TJ Hughes. They were comfortable, and smart enough in case someone came to the door, and also for church.

Neat rows of plants in several different colours had been

planted in the soil around the lawn, their hues repeating in the same order all the way around. A trellis, where there had once been a solid fence, allowed Lomond and Donna to see through to the back garden, which was equally well-kept. The large living room window, which used to have the same permanently shut Venetian blinds as the other houses, was now framed by elegant lace curtains, allowing sunlight to fill the room.

As Brenda prepared herself for her unknown guests, Lomond said, 'We should have a quick word about what to expect in there. We're about to take away the one thing that lady's been clinging onto since her daughter disappeared.'

Donna nodded solemnly.

'Whatever you do,' said Lomond, 'temper expectations. Even if Lianne had only disappeared last month, this would be a hard task.'

'I know,' Donna agreed, looking towards the house.

'You've not had to do this before, have you?'

'Yeah...I mean, in training.'

'No, I mean for real, Donna. You're about to sit in front of someone who realises one of the people they love the most in the world is dead. It's easy to lose discipline and forget you're there to deliver information. Not to deliver empty promises.'

Donna nodded again like she'd been there before. 'I remember training, boss.'

Lomond turned towards her. 'You're hearing me, but you're not listening, Donna. You think you know what to expect. Trust me, you have no idea what you're about to feel in there.'

Lomond knew that having issued the warning, it was his job to now build her back up. To remind her she can handle it. She had done the training, run all the mocks back in Mill Street where she had prepped to go into Family Liaison, and there was no one else on his team he'd rather be in that room with.

She took a deep breath, then nodded again.

For the first time, Lomond realised how nervous she actually was. And how well she had hidden it until now – a trait that came from years of living in an abusive childhood home.

Brenda Gribbin watched Lomond and Donna approach, almost hiding behind the living room door. She recognised Lomond, despite how much time had passed.

As Lomond reached out to chap the door, he got a flashback of what his last meeting there had been like.

When Brenda opened the door, it was like it was twenty years ago all over again...

CHAPTER NINE

20 YEARS AGO

Brenda Gribbin opened the door, wearing the dressing gown she'd been wrapped in for the past twelve hours – another sleepless night. Her eyes were red raw from tears.

Lomond said, 'Mrs Gribbin? Detective Sergeant John Lomond. You can call me John.'

The woman next to him showed her a Strathclyde Police ID. 'Detective Inspector Linda Boyle,' she said. 'Nice to meet you.'

Brenda was too distraught to be aware of it, but subconsciously she warmed to Lomond more instantly. His eye contact was unwavering, and he had a sympathetic expression. His voice softer than his colleagues. Linda's voice was harsh, barely changed from the usual brusque tone of hers that permeated Pitt Street CID. Even her way of saying 'nice to meet you' made it sound somehow like a threat.

Linda's eyes were everywhere when they entered, assessing, judging everything. The mess. The clutter. The fact that the husband was still out in the garden shed and hadn't come to introduce himself yet.

Brenda had to call out to him from the back door. Her voice tired, depleted. She'd been calling on him for decades, and she knew that she'd probably be doing the same decades from now.

Lomond sat down the way most police sat on people's sofas: near the front, legs splayed. It wasn't businesslike to sit back on a sofa when there were questions to be asked. He rubbed at the front of his head, where his hair had been receding of late. It was still clinging on around the back and sides. But on top it was fading fast.

'Can I get you a tea? Coffee?' Brenda asked.

Linda refused, quickly. She didn't want to spend any longer there than was necessary. She gave a little micro-expression of irritation when Lomond took up the offer of coffee.

While she was gone in the kitchen, Linda and Lomond could make out murmured disagreement as mugs chinked on the worktop and the kettle boiled.

When Brenda returned with coffee for Lomond, she brought her husband Jimmy in tow.

He was dressed in an old golf polo shirt and blue jeans, embarrassed to be sitting with two police detectives while his wife was wearing her dressing gown, clearly not dressed for the day.

The living room was full of photographs of the family. Brenda and Jimmy's wedding. Family photographs. Lianne as a baby, then a little girl. The usual Catholic ones. Baptism. First Communion. Then Lianne as a young lady, where the expression had darkened significantly. The smile of the early years long gone.

Linda stared at a framed picture on the wall. It said "*LIVE LOVE LAUGH*".

'She got that for me,' Brenda said, then corrected herself. 'Us. The picture.'

Jimmy took a seat, barely making eye contact. 'I'm Jimmy.'

Pursed lips and nods from Lomond and Linda.

'Do youse want any biscuits?' Brenda asked, then immediately turned to Jimmy. 'Get some biscuits, would you, Jim? No' the digestives or Abernethys. The Jaffa cakes in the cupboard.'

'Really,' Lomond began, 'we're fine, Mrs Gribbin.'

'It's Brenda,' she said. 'It's no bother.' She lowered her voice once Jimmy had left the room. 'He prefers to keep himself busy. He's been like that since... Spending a lot more time in his shed than usual.'

'That's understandable,' said Lomond. 'We all cope with these things in different ways.'

Eager to press on, Linda said, 'Mrs Gribbin, you mentioned on the phone that there were some things you thought we should know about Lianne.'

Brenda leaned forward to check if Jimmy was coming back yet. There was no sign.

He was, in fact, waiting silently in the kitchen, holding a plate of Jaffa cakes. He'd heard the question. And he knew the answer.

Brenda said, 'It's about Lianne's...line of work. You see...' She took a deep breath, and cleared her throat nervously. 'She'd...she's been working...as a prostitute.'

'I see,' Linda replied.

'I would have told you sooner when I reported her missing...but I was...' She tried to think of any other word to use, but couldn't. 'I was ashamed. But I thought it might help if you knew.'

'It is helpful to know that,' Lomond said.

After a number of logistical questions surrounding anyone Lianne knew who might be of help, Brenda admitted that neither she nor Jimmy knew anyone in Lianne's life now.

Lomond said, 'May I ask, are there drugs involved currently in Lianne's...lifestyle?'

Brenda nodded, eyes closed.

'Brenda, Lianne's been missing for eight days now. As we said back at the station, the first week can be crucial in locating someone. Is there anyone you think she might be with? Anyone she might have gone to?'

Jimmy reappeared with the Jaffa cakes. 'Well, there's the Rafferty boy,' he said, clearly unimpressed. 'But you know about him.'

'We're struggling to locate him too,' Linda said.

'We don't have any address for him, do we Brenda?'

'No,' she replied. 'Lianne knew we didn't like him. She always had such terrible taste in boys. Always so rough. She deserved better. She was a happy girl growing up. Then when she became a teenager she just changed. Almost overnight. She never used to care what people thought of her. Her clothes. Or anything like that. Didn't mind being uncool. Then slowly, she stopped laughing as much. Became withdrawn.'

Lomond and Linda exchanged a glance, thinking the same thing. Textbook signs of childhood sexual abuse. Sudden changes in mood or personality. Anxiety. Social withdrawal.

'Drugs came next,' said Brenda. 'Then going about with boys...' She choked back tears. 'I found her...' She could barely speak now. The presence of Jimmy during the retelling of the story was making her uncomfortable.

Jimmy leaned forward, unconsciously mirroring Lomond's body language. He didn't know where to look.

Brenda continued, 'I found her...you know...on her knees, in the back lane behind the garden. A guy as old as you.'

'How old was she at time?' Lomond asked.

'Fifteen.'

'Did you report it?' asked Linda.

'No.'

'Did you see her with him again?'

'No,' Brenda said. 'I shouted for Jimmy, and he ran after him. I think that kept him away for good. That was just the start.' She began to cry again. 'She was never mine again after that...'

Jimmy looked down the length of the sofa at her, and passed a tissue. He then dropped a thick hand on her leg.

Consulting his notes, Lomond said, 'And the last time you heard from Lianne was...Sunday. Is that right?'

'That's right. Come hell or high water, she always called me on a Sunday night. Just a wee natter, you know. What had been on the telly, what I was having for my dinner, what was she having for her dinner. She knew we disapproved of what she did, that we wanted her to do something safer...'

'That junk,' Jimmy spat. 'That's what done it. Filling her arm with that rubbish. That's what's to blame here.'

'That may be so,' Lomond ventured. 'But our first priority is to ensure that Lianne is safe...' He glanced at Linda again. 'I should warn you that the circumstances of Lianne's disappearance leave us concerned that she may have come to some harm...'

Brenda's face creased, her thoughts straying to that which she and Jimmy had been trying to fend off since the police classed her as a missing person.

Lomond continued, 'We've checked the records with the pharmacy where she has been collecting her methadone. It's now eight days since she last collected that. And we know that methadone had been a daily routine for her.' He glanced at Linda again for guidance, but couldn't tell if Linda thought he was doing fine or not. He held his hands out, turning palms up.

'Look, we're going to leave no stone unturned to try and find her. And we're all hoping that she's just been staying with someone else for a while, gone off the grid.' He paused, as Linda had told him to. 'But at the same point, considering the time frames we're dealing with here, there is a chance that the worst may well have happened. And you should prepare yourselves for that.'

Jimmy showed no emotion. Like nothing at all had been said.

'It's John isn't it?' said Brenda.

'That's right,' he replied.

Brenda inched forward in her seat. 'Promise me you'll find her.'

Linda made some polite noises that it was just about being realistic, and it was still quite early in the investigation, and it was only sensible to temper expectations.

When it came time to leave, Lomond wanted to say something, but didn't. Something about Linda's presence put him off.

OUTSIDE, the garden was in as much disarray as Lomond's thoughts.

The paving slabs were broken and at wonky angles. No plants, just empty soil ringing around the uncut lawn. Conifers beside the house were messy and overgrown, lost all their shape. And the view to the side of the house and to the back garden was blocked at the front by a solid wooden fence too tall to see over.

Once they were in the car, Lomond patted himself down.

'What have you lost?' Linda asked.

'Damn,' said Lomond. 'I left my pen. Let me nip back for it.'

Linda didn't say anything, but she suspected she knew what was happening by the front door while Lomond was alone with Brenda.

When he got back in the car, Linda asked, 'Did you get your pen?'

'Aye,' he replied. 'Fell down the couch.'

She paused. 'Show me.'

Lomond froze. 'Eh?'

'Can you show me the pen you went back in to get?'

Lomond faced the windscreen, wanting to look anywhere but her face.

'What did you promise her, John?'

He picked absentmindedly at a bit of lint on his trouser leg. 'The bare minimum,' he replied.

'Try me with specifics.'

'I told her we'd get her daughter back safely.'

Linda sighed. 'You don't make someone like that promises, John. Ever'

He turned to face her. 'Why not?'

'Lianne Gribbin's been missing for eight days now. Do you know how few people turn up again after going missing eight days? Out of nine thousand people a year who go missing, almost all of them show up after four days. Of the ones who don't and just want to vanish into thin air and start a new life, one per cent of that nine thousand show up dead. That's ninety people.'

'Thank you for the maths lesson,' Lomond sniped.

'My point is that of those ninety who turn up dead, Glasgow has to deal with over half of them. The sad truth is that Lianne Gribbin is probably lying passed out somewhere with a needle in her arm, or she's disappeared to start again in Edinburgh, or she's dead. That's what the statistics say. That's why making promises to a worried mum isn't smart.'

'She needs hope right now.'

'No,' Linda fired back, 'what she needs is her daughter back, John. And if you and Eilidh were in her shoes I'm pretty sure you'd agree.'

'It's a bit soon for me to be talking to Eilidh about that kind of thing.'

'If I can give you any advice on the subject, do it sooner rather than later. Because if you want to progress the way you say you do, the more you see in this job, the less you might want to do it.'

'There's always time.'

'No, there's not actually. We're going to blink, and before you know it whole decades are going to have passed,' she snapped her fingers, 'like that.'

CHAPTER TEN

When Brenda opened the door, she looked like an entirely different woman. Not least because she had aged – though the years had been kind to her. Her face said it all. Acceptance. Commiseration.

There was no other reason for a police visit – certainly not from a Detective Chief Inspector – unless the worst had finally been confirmed.

'Do you remember me, Mrs Gribbin?' Lomond asked.

She snorted. 'Of course I remember you, John.'

'I think we should maybe go inside.'

That was when Brenda knew what had happened.

The contrasts to the previous version of the house were clear to see. All the clutter was gone. The house was so bare, Lomond thought for a moment that Brenda might be moving house soon. The *LIVE LAUGH LOVE* sign was gone. Now replaced by a large gold crucifix.

The most notable addition to the hall was a home stoup – a font for holy water – on the wall by the front door. A porcelain angel holding a white bowl that had water in it. On the sideboard was what looked like an ordinary water bottle. One litre. But the sticker on front looked strange. Closer inspection revealed it to be from Lourdes. Or so the sticker claimed.

Unsure if they were about to offend some Catholic sensibility, Donna whispered, 'Do we bless ourselves?'

Lomond shook his head, no.

Brenda gestured to the stoup. 'You know you can buy it online now. The holy water. It's great. It comes pre-blessed.'

Lomond didn't have the heart to tell her that it had probably been filled from a tap in an industrial estate some place.

Holy water had fascinated Lomond since his school days. A friend's sick mother had visited Lourdes once and returned with half a dozen tankards of holy water from the Sanctuary. It was free. Although there was a near-industrial set up of a long silver pipe with dozens of taps attached to accommodate the long queues as people filled up bottles. His pal's mum had hoarded the stuff like canned goods for a fallout shelter.

For all the good it had done her, Lomond couldn't help but wonder if Brenda had kept receipts for the water, considering the news they'd come to deliver.

In the living room, only pictures of Lianne remained. There were no marriage photos or family holiday pictures anymore.

Brenda was on the verge of tears when they sat down. Voice trembling, hands shaking. She swallowed hard, trying to compose herself. It had taken twenty years to feel this. She dreaded to call it something as callous as relief. But that's what she needed. To be *relieved* of grief. Wanting to make Lomond's task a little easier, she asked, 'Have you found her?'

Lomond sat on the couch the same way he had all those years ago. On the edge. Elbows resting on splayed legs. He nodded sombrely. 'We believe so, Brenda. I'm very sorry.'

Having finally been given permission to let go of everything she'd been hanging onto, Brenda started to cry.

Lomond couldn't sit and wait. They could have been sitting there for several minutes until she managed to compose herself again. While Brenda sobbed, Lomond explained, 'Donna's going to talk you through what's led us here this morning. Okay?' He didn't expect a response.

Donna tried to stick to the script, but only now did she understand what Lomond had tried to warn her about. Relaying the information at hand while someone's life falls apart in real-time in front of you, is no easy task.

Donna explained, 'Early this morning, we received a call from Fallon Construction about the discovery of human remains on a site next to the River Clyde at Water Row on the Govan side. Preliminary examination of the scene has suggested that the remains are Lianne's.'

As Lomond had instructed, Donna paused to let the news sink in. But also to let Brenda ask questions. In Lomond's experience, it made it feel more like a conversation that way, rather than a monologue being delivered. In his early days, he'd delivered such news like a monologue, when his senior officer told him it was best to get it over and done with, by providing all the facts at once. But over time Lomond noticed that on the human level it always failed. As soon as he told someone their loved one was dead, they couldn't hear anything else for a while.

Brenda eventually managed to ask, 'What makes you sure enough that you've come here to tell me?'

Lomond explained about the pendant.

Brenda nodded. 'Will I be able to get it back?'

'Soon,' Lomond answered. 'Very soon. I'll make sure of it. But first we have to run tests on everything we have. Given the time frames involved, this requires dental records.'

Brenda nodded curtly. 'I always knew this day would come eventually. After five years I forced herself to start smiling again. To continue with life. I found my faith again. After Jimmy died. I did all the things people expect you to do after a period of grieving. Because I had to behave like Lianne was dead. I didn't know that she'd ever be found, and I didn't want to miss my chance to grieve for her properly. But still, even after all that, you can't help clinging on to a little bit of hope.' She looked up, wiping her tears away. 'Your promise back then gave me a little bit of hope. Do you know that?'

Lomond almost seemed embarrassed, reliving the episode in his head. 'It wasn't professional of me.'

'You've got nothing to apologise for, John.'

Donna was fascinated by the version of John Lomond sitting next to her. It was a more vulnerable Lomond than she had ever seen before.

CHAPTER ELEVEN

Lomond explained, 'On police dramas, there's always that scene where the cop who made a promise to find someone has to go back and deliver bad news. I think those scenes exist, because things like this really happen.' He gestured back and forth to Brenda. 'Life happens. Promises get broken. And I'm sorry that I've been unable to keep the promise I made to you.'

Brenda replied, 'I wasn't naive back then. I appreciated the hope it gave me. I needed it actually. I'm not going to kick and stamp my feet because you promised you'd bring her back to me, and you haven't. As if promising something like that is all it takes. It's not that simple. That tiny speck of hope that someday the phone will ring, or the door will get chapped is what keeps you going in all those dark moments. I looked up the statistics when she went missing. The...' She broke off, failing to remember. 'What do you call that officer who comes around and sits with you to answer questions?'

'Family liaison officer,' Donna answered.

'Yeah, that guy. He was nice. I asked him, and he told me honestly what happens to folk who go missing. I thought, fair enough. He didn't want to lie to me. But you never lied to me either, John.'

'I did ev–' He couldn't bring himself to say it.

Brenda finished it for him. 'Everything you could?'

Lomond cleared his throat, considering whether he should say it or not. Whether it would help, or cause more pain. But his relationship with Brenda Gribbin didn't feel like the usual. 'I didn't do everything I could,' he admitted. 'Strathclyde Police didn't. When I was told to move on to a different enquiry, I did. We all did. Lianne was forgotten. She fell between the cracks like so many people.'

'It's not just you,' said Brenda. 'I failed as well. When we had Lianne, I knew that being a mum was what I was meant to do. To be responsible for someone. Helping them grow up. When I think of what Lianne fell into, you can't call that anything else but a failure.'

Lomond was adamant. 'You didn't fail.'

'No, you didn't,' Donna added.

'Did you ever have kids, John?' asked Brenda.

He paused. By the look on his face the question hadn't stirred any particular emotion inside him. But inside, his heart had turned black and his veins dried up. It was hard to keep bereavement at bay on a daily basis with how suddenly and violently thoughts of his loss could intrude into his life. Like a grand piano falling through a ceiling.

He answered, 'No.'

'When your kid ends up a drug addict and working on the streets, believe me, you've failed.'

'It wasn't anything you did. Lianne had a complicated life.'

'I wasn't there for her. And now it's too late.'

While Donna consoled her, Lomond said, 'Can I get you anything, Brenda?'

Wiping her nose with a tissue that had been stuffed up her sleeve – a habit instilled in her by her mother – she answered, 'A cup of tea would be nice.'

The kitchen was as immaculate as the living room. Even the minor mess created by making a cup of tea seemed to lower the tone of the room significantly.

It was while the kettle boiled, and Donna and Brenda talked in the living room, that Lomond's gaze landed on the shed outside.

He couldn't help but remember his and Linda's shared look when Lianne's distressed teenage years had been discussed.

With the kettle on a loud rolling boil, Lomond took his opportunity. He sneaked out the kitchen and headed for the garden shed. It was the only place on the property that hadn't been maintained properly through the years. Everything else had been painted, repaired, or replaced. But not the shed. It was dilapidated. Moss-strewn on top.

It was also the place that he knew Jimmy Gribbin spent the most time. Ever since the initial missing person enquiry, Lomond had been unable to shake the image of Jimmy out in the shed as they had arrived. What had been of such immediate concern to him in the shed in such a situation?

Lomond turned the door handle. It gave instantly, unlocked. Once he went inside he could tell why. There was nothing of any value in there. Just rusting old tools on a workbench. Everything covered in cobwebs. Including a framed portrait of a horse nailed to the wooden wall. Lomond stared at it. It was an impressionistic, hazy charcoal drawing. A print.

Then something underneath the workbench caught his eye.

He pulled out the metal drawer, brushing away the cobwebs and thick dust with the back of his hand.

'I'll be damned,' he said to himself.

He picked up the item in the drawer. A heavy horse's bridle in black leather. Then, buried underneath, was an old photograph. In it, was a much younger Jimmy Gribbin. In his late forties, Lomond guessed. He was standing in the middle of a group of children who were crouched down in front of a black horse in the middle of a field somewhere. In the background was a crooked oak tree. And the corner of a building that Lomond couldn't work out what it was. Something that struck him was the expressions on the children's faces. None of them were smiling. They were a mixture of ages, ranging from about five all the way through to mid-teens.

Then Lomond remembered the kettle. It would have boiled by now.

He shoved the photo into his pocket, and closed the drawer with the bridle in it.

When he got back to the kitchen, Brenda was already on her way through.

Lomond rushed across to the kettle, appearing to have been standing there all the time.

'Did you find everything okay?' she asked.

'I did, thanks,' he replied, handing her a cup of tea.

As they said their goodbyes at the front door a short while later, Lomond said, 'We'll be in touch, Brenda. And if there's anything you need, day or night, you can call me.' He handed her his card.

'Thank you, John,' she said, producing Donna's card which she already had. 'Donna said the same.'

'Good,' he replied, then noticed a strange moment between Donna and Brenda.

Something more than a mere look. There was intimacy behind it. Solemnity on Donna's part.

Holding Donna's card up, Brenda said, 'I'm going to hold you to that.'

Donna's face turned ashen. Like a child caught out in a lie.

Lomond said nothing. He let her suffer in silence as he walked slowly around the back of the car to get to the driver's seat.

Donna shut her eyes in the passenger seat. Before Lomond could say anything, she opened her eyes. 'In this order,' she said, 'I know. You warned me. I didn't believe you. I fucked up. And you were right.'

Lomond explained, 'Donna, I've seen so many things in my career. You haven't seen even a percentage of that. I know what I'm talking about. That's why I tried to–'

'I know.' She shut her eyes again briefly. 'You heard what she said about hope. The hope of finding Lianne is gone. I thought let's at least give her some hope that we can now get justice for her memory.'

Lomond replied, 'Hope is a dangerous thing to throw around, Donna. You need to be careful how you handle hope. That hope you gave Brenda is about as useless as windows on a submarine.'

'I don't believe that. And I don't think *you* really believe that either. I kept hearing from all the old timers at Mill Street, oh aye, don't get too close to anyone. Don't get emotionally involved, that's a mug's game...We don't have to just be the ones who deliver bad news. That if we show up the worst has already happened. We can still do good in this job. I think you believe that too. Somewhere.'

Lomond started the engine.

Donna stared at him.

'What is it?' he asked.

'Are you going to tell me what you were doing in the shed?'

'You saw that?'

'If I hadn't redirected Brenda, she would have caught you.'

He didn't speak until they had pulled away from the kerb. 'It's the dad. Jimmy. I think we need to do some digging.'

CHAPTER TWELVE

Pardeep and Jason were heading along the M74 to the city's fringes on the south-east. The motorway skirting between Dalmarnock and Rutherglen, where the city lost all of its height and a lot of its density.

In its place was a seemingly endless sea of warehouses. If the city centre was Glasgow's heart and brain, the south-east was its calloused hands. An area where nothing really connected coherently, but when put together formed much of what kept the city going. Plumbers. Glazing. Wholesalers. Tool hire. Storage. Car bodyshops. Then, at the opposite end of the spectrum, there was a gigantic warehouse playground full of trampolines sat right by the motorway's edge, not far from the country's biggest golf driving range, whose perimeter nets stretched so high into the air they could be seen from half a mile away.

'It's only a matter of time before that thing snags an aeroplane,' Pardeep remarked as they drove past.

Jason was too concerned with the file on Thomas Rafferty. 'He's a real piece of work this guy.'

'How bad?'

'A bit of everything. Goes all the way back to eighteen years old.'

'Much in the way of escalation?'

'Not really. Looks like he's just been a bit of a dick for a while. Burglary. Minor drugs offences. Assault. Nothing harrowing. Until this thing last year. By miles the most serious offence.'

'What exactly happened?' asked Pardeep.

'A prostitute reported that he attempted to snatch her off the street by pulling her into his car.'

Pardeep paused, giving the report a glance of curiosity. 'What kind of car?'

'Not a white saloon like from the Lianne Gribbin file, if that's what you're thinking.'

Pardeep sighed in disappointment.

Having cut his teeth as a detective constable in some of the vice-ridden areas in the city, Pardeep had experience with many of the dangers that prostitutes faced on a nightly basis. But he had never heard of anyone attempting a snatch.

His eyes narrowed. 'Any history of soliciting?'

Jason did a quick sweep through Rafferty's records. 'Nothing.' Something appeared to hold Jason's interest on the page.

'What is it?' asked Pardeep.

'It's probably nothing but...the interview transcript from after his arrest. He was asked why he tried to abduct the woman.'

'What did he say?'

'He said "I won't answer that." He had a lawyer present. Why didn't he just say no comment?'

'It was probably some trainee lawyer that was sent in, didn't know what he was doing.'

'It's a strange choice of words. Like there was an explanation, but he didn't want to give it.'

Doubts already raised, Pardeep knew that the arrest at least warranted talking to the guy. But his attention was being stolen by something else.

Jason caught him eyeing something in the rear-view mirror. He was about to turn around to look out the back window.

Pardeep stopped him. 'No no no, eyes forward. I don't want him knowing I've clocked him. Mirror.'

Jason checked his mirror and saw a beat-up, rusting silver saloon behind them – just too far away to make out a registration plate.

Pardeep said, 'He's been tailing us since we left the station.'

'It's not that far, man,' said Jason. 'In any case, who would be following us?'

'I've no idea, but he is definitely following us. Remember I took a wrong turn and came off the M8 at Kinning Park, like I was going home? If this guy was bound for this direction on the M74, that's a hell of a coincidence he took a wrong turn as well. He should have just stayed on the motorway.'

'Slow right down. See if he comes past.'

Pardeep went all the way down to forty miles an hour, enough to prompt horn blasts from further back, forcing an articulated lorry to overtake them. They took the Cambuslang turnoff, next to the driving range.

'See,' said Jason, as the silver car continued on. 'It's nothing. You've been watching too much *Line of Duty* again. Seeing conspiracies everywhere.'

The silver car peeled off into the middle lane and sped away.

Pardeep and Jason were too far down the slip road to get

eyes on the driver. But Pardeep caught a glimpse of the end of the registration plate: NGY.

THE CAR WASH was situated between the M74 flyover at the railway bridge on Cambuslang Road, adjacent to budget kitchen and bathroom showrooms and a container storage facility. It was a prime location, on the main route towards East Kilbride for those coming from Glasgow, making it one of the busiest car washes in the city. A highly efficient production line was set up to handle each step, from the first rinse to the final polish. Formerly a petrol station, the old forecourt provided an ideal covered space for washing cars in all weather conditions. It was never quiet.

Pardeep couldn't even find a spot to park on the forecourt and had to abandon his car by mounting the pavement. Meanwhile, Jason, having found his stride with MIT, interrupted a lad of about nineteen who was hosing down a car covered in foam.

'Where's your gaffer?' Jason asked.

'Office,' came the distracted response.

Pardeep tapped Jason on the arm, indicating Thomas Rafferty across the forecourt, applying a foam hose to a van. If Rafferty had noticed them, he didn't show it.

A man with an olive complexion and wearing a puffy jacket and a woolly hat despite it being twelve degrees outside, was halfway through a Subway sandwich.

He immediately frowned at the two officers. In a thick Arabic-sounding accent, he said, 'What you want, guys?'

The pair showed their IDs.

'Fuck's sake,' the man complained. 'What now? Is that

bitch still banging on about her mini-valet? I told her, prices advertised are "From". *From*!' He threw his hand up theatrically. 'Take me to court, why don't you? See if I fucking care.'

'Sir,' Pardeep took delight in explaining. 'Officers from Major Investigations don't follow up on car wash mini-valet complaints.'

'Then what do you want?'

Jason showed the man Rafferty's mugshot.

Pardeep said, 'We need to speak to Thomas Rafferty.'

The manager turned back towards his office. 'He'll be done in five minutes. He's got three more cars to foam.'

Pardeep chuckled. 'What's your name, please?'

The man hesitated. 'Amir.'

'Amir, I'm a Detective Constable on a murder enquiry.'

Amir's complexion suddenly turned paler as he shot a worried look towards Rafferty.

Pardeep said, 'Get him over here now. Or I could come back with Immigration Enforcement, who can check all your employees' paperwork.' He added, 'Which I'm sure is all in order. Because you won't be paying anyone here cash-in-hand.' He paused. 'Will you?'

Amir turned, reluctantly, and shouted, 'Tommy! These guys want to talk to you.'

There was nothing in Rafferty's reaction that suggested he might run. It was rather the look of a man who wished he had seen the last of the police.

Pardeep and Jason waited for him outside the manager's office, then led him around the side of the building next to tall piles of tyres.

Rafferty was thin with a pasty complexion. His lips were so thin they almost weren't there. His eyes too big for his rat-like face, emphasised by his shaved head, and pointy ears that could have been used as letter openers.

'Whit is it?' he spat with full-on neddy contempt.

He still looked young for being in his early forties, and it wasn't hard to imagine him tearing about some housing estate on a motorised scooter, causing chaos with his pals close behind, dressed in tracksuits and getting in fights every single day.

Jason explained, 'Thomas, we're here to talk to you about what happened last year with you and Paula McMeekin.'

He scowled. 'I did ma time, ya pricks. Whit aboot it?'

Pardeep stepped in, having had a little more experience with hardcore neds like Rafferty. 'We're also here about Lianne Gribbin.'

The veil of Rafferty's aggression suddenly fell away. Almost tenderly, he asked, 'Whit about her?'

'I'm afraid it appears that Lianne's remains have been found near the banks of the River Clyde.'

Rafferty's chin wobbled. He looked down, then back up. He sniffed away a tear. 'Whereabouts?'

'The Govan area.'

Rafferty nodded. 'She's deid?'

'We don't have confirmation identifying the victim. But I'm pretty sure it's her. There's some jewellery of hers around the neck.'

He turned away, putting his head in his hands, then seemed to fight back against the vulnerability in his pose. Instead, he ran his hands viciously over his head, as if trying to shake the news away. He then relented, cradling his head in his hands, like a footballer who had missed an important shot on goal, then he yelled out primitively, 'Fuck!'

Pardeep and Jason left him to process the news in his own way.

Trying to draw him back in, Pardeep said, 'You two were together when she disappeared?'

When Rafferty turned around again he had tears in his eyes. 'Yeah. I mean, kind of...' He dropped down to the ground, taking a seat on the kerb. 'Ah fuckin' tried tae tell youse,' he cried. 'Ah telt youse somebody did her in. Instead youse wasted yer time searchin' ma fuckin' gaff.'

'Was there anyone else you suspected of being involved in Lianne's disappearance?'

'Ah fuckin' said,' Rafferty complained, but calmly this time. 'An' nae cunt believed me. So fuckin' well done, eh? Fuckin' well done.'

'Thomas,' Pardeep explained, taking a seat next to him. 'We need to speak to you – off the record, you know – because this charge last year, I mean, it doesn't look good for you, does it? You were the boyfriend of a prostitute who turns up dead after all these years. And you've not long been caught trying to snatch one off the street. I'm just saying, it doesn't look good. But we–' Pardeep gestured to himself and Jason, 'we just want to hear your side of things.'

Rafferty huffed, taking out a cigarette as fast as he could. As if he couldn't continue breathing without one.

Jason was about to sit down on the other side of Rafferty, but Pardeep shook his head at him. He didn't want Rafferty feeling hemmed in.

'We'd had a fight,' Rafferty explained.

'Over what?' Pardeep asked.

'We were just kids when we got th'gether. When she started gaming, I stopped wantin' tae kiss her. She telt me she didnae dae that wae the punters, you know. Kissin' on the mouth. It was, like, wan of their rules. Anyways, wan night I found messages fae some guy.'

'There's nothing in the original missing person file about that. Did you tell anyone?'

'Mate, I've spent the last twenty years tryin' tae forget it aw.'

Jason asked, 'Did you know who the guy was?'

Rafferty answered, 'Some older guy wi a fuckin' weird name.'

'Who was it?'

'I dunno. She wouldnae tell me. But the messages I seen, I think it was an older guy.'

'What makes you say that?'

'Just the patter, you know?' Rafferty looked up and away. 'What was his name?'

Jason, looking out towards the street, said softly, 'Pardeep?'

Pardeep raised his hand to indicate *not now*.

Rafferty wittered on, 'Was it Winston? Or Wilbur or some shit?'

Jason waved his hand in Pardeep's face. 'Pardeep, he's back...'

Across the road, the silver saloon was idling, but the moment the driver spotted Jason, he sped off.

Acting on impulse, Jason tore off after him. Then remembered he didn't have car keys.

Pardeep launched them at him from a distance, like an American football quarterback, straight into Jason's waiting hands.

He started up the engine then stamped on the accelerator, nearly getting T-boned by a Luton van entering the car wash. 'Shit,' Jason cursed, having to reverse to make space to turn. But he did so at speed, then launched the car across the busy road, to a cacophony of horns. Somehow he managed to clear the first lane, thanks to a quick-witted taxi driver's emergency stop. But making it all the way across to the other lane was too much. The traffic wouldn't yield.

Within a few seconds, the silver saloon was away under the railway bridge, from where there were about a dozen different directions to choose from.

Jason called it in. 'I need a trace on a silver Hyundai, registration ending NGY. Could be heading west along the M74 from Rutherglen junction two.'

CHAPTER THIRTEEN

THE HOSTEL WAS in the heart of Polmadie on the south side of Glasgow. Not known as one of the picturesque parts of the city, it could charitably be described as rough. There seemed to be an off licence on every street corner, a grim example of the free market fulfilling demand. Most of the houses were old. Not many developers had the rose-tinted glasses to see a bright future in the area.

Off the main Polmadie Road, sandwiched between a cash and carry, and a taxi depot, was the Woman's Action Refuge hostel, known as Copeland House. The accidental acronym of WAR was appropriate at nighttime. But during the day, it was quiet outside, unrecognisable from what it could become later.

It was a two-floor former office block, converted in the early 2000s as a hostel for at-risk women. Tragically, it was full every single night of the year, and had been since opening.

On the way in, a young woman dressed in the clothes of the previous night held her phone out, talking on speaker. Clearly intoxicated, she leaned against a concrete stanchion placed there to prevent traffic mounting the pavement and parking outside the main doors of the hostel. Her eye makeup had run down onto her cheeks. The male voice at the other end was loud and aggressive.

Ross slowed as they approached, but Willie quickly encouraged him.

'Come on,' he insisted.

As soon as they entered the lobby, an overwhelming smell of damp and stale alcohol hit the two officers. The decor was dated, and everywhere the men looked the place was in a state of disrepair. Crumbling plaster and mouldings, the stone staircase next to the reception desk decaying. The porcelain floor tiles were stained and broken, and clearly hadn't seen so much as a mop in years.

The manager resided – or possibly hid – behind a plastic screen window like a receptionist at a dentist. As soon as he saw Ross and Willie he rose from his office chair. He knew exactly what detectives look like, and how they carry themselves.

After introducing themselves, Willie said, 'We're trying to get any information you might have on a former resident.'

The manager slid the clear screen aside, unleashing a wave of body odour that nearly knocked Willie and Ross on their backs.

'Name?' the manager asked with bored impatience.

'Lianne Gribbin.'

'Never heard of her.' The manager attempted to slide the screen shut.

Willie reached out and stopped him. 'What's your name?'

The manager paused. He was skinny and unshaven, with a rounded back from sitting with bad posture for years in that very office. He was missing his two front teeth, and his brown cardigan had a week's worth of dandruff on the shoulders. 'Archie,' he said.

'How long you worked here, Archie?' Willie asked.

'I've been here since day one,' he replied.

'Then working in a place like this, you must know how it works. We can come back with a warrant–'

Archie tutted, then turned to an ancient computer on the desk behind him. 'Hold on...' The keyboard was missing keys, and it was covered in coffee stains. Dust and skin flakes had built up so much over the years, it was visible between all the keys. 'Police are always showing up around here asking for people past and present.'

Willie said, 'I don't know how far back your computer records go, but Lianne Gribbin went missing twenty years ago.'

Archie backed away from the computer, then crouched down under the desk. After browsing racks of red binder files, he pulled out one marked with the date of twenty years ago.

'You keep everything?' Ross asked.

'Like I said,' Archie replied. 'You never know. Most of these women, they're not in a good way. Sometimes bad things happen to them. I know this isn't exactly the Hilton, but I do my best to keep them safe.' He dropped the heavy binder down on the table and put on a pair of reading glasses with greasy fingerprints all over the lenses. They perched on the end of Archie's nose as he consulted the dates on the top of the pages. 'What month?' he asked.

'April,' Ross answered, giving the last month that Lianne had been seen.

With the layout of the pages burned into his brain, Archie soon found the name. He spun the binder around to Willie and Ross. 'That's the sign-in book for residents and any visitors.

Apart from police, every single person through that door,' he pointed to the main doors, 'signs in here.'

Willie scanned through the names, then pointed at one. 'What about this? Walter Murdock.'

Archie stared at the name, a hint of recognition appearing on his face. He squinted, then looked up at Willie. 'Got a photo of her?'

Willie took out his phone, and showed Archie a picture of Lianne. The one used on all their missing person documentation.

Archie squinted. 'I remember this one. The fella...Walter, he came back a lot, look...' He reached over to the binder and found several instances of Walter Murdock signing in to visit.

Ross, noting the lengthy gaps between signing in and out, said, 'How long are visitors are allowed to stay? Because this guy never stays for less than half an hour.'

Archie sighed, and removed his glasses. 'Look...I run a straight up place here. Whatever a resident gets up to in her room isn't my business. I'm not here to tell folk they shouldn't drink or inject or...whatever else they want to do. I put a roof over their heads and keep them out of trouble for a little while. That's it. When Lianne first went missing, you lot came round here asking questions. I tried to tell the officer about this guy Murdock.'

Willie asked, 'What did you try to tell him? Did he seem suspicious in any way to you?'

'Only in the sense that he obviously had no business being in a place like this with a woman like her.'

'What do you mean?'

'He was well-dressed. Well-spoken. Posh, you know. I didn't think much of it at first. I thought he was maybe paying her so he could have a wee bit of rough. You get that with some of the punters. They're from nice areas. Maybe they want to feel superior or something, I don't know. Or they think it's easier to get away with paying for it round places like this. But the Murdock guy, he wasn't like the others. It seemed like he was trying to help her. They had a big chat down here one time. He was trying to give her money and she refused to take it. Not something I see very often round here, folk refusing money, so it stuck in my head. When the officer came round asking about Lianne, I tried to tell him about Murdock, but he wouldn't listen. I kept checking the newspapers at the time, and when I never seen anything come up, I went to the station to report it, you know. About all the visits, in case this guy had done something.'

'What happened?' asked Willie.

Archie scoffed. 'Nothing happened! I spoke to a constable who said he'd take a statement. Then the same officer who came here came out the front desk and sent me away. Said it was all fine. That the Lianne girl had shown up and it was all over.'

Both Willie and Ross had the same stunned expression.

'As in, she'd been found?' said Willie.

'That's what he told me,' Archie replied. Then he paused. 'Wasn't she found?'

Glossing over the question, Ross asked, 'Do you remember the officer's name or rank?'

Archie shrugged. 'This was a long, long time ago, you know. He wasn't uniform, mind. He wore a suit. Posh sort, you know. Hoity toity. Dismissive. But I couldn't tell you his name. I've got a good memory, but...' He shrugged, then noticed the cleaner trudging past with a battered old Henry hoover. 'Margaret,' he called out, leaning through the window. 'Do you remember this woman?'

Willie showed her a picture of Lianne on his phone.

Margaret shook her head like her time was being wasted. 'I already spoke to the detective sergeant or inspector or whatever about her.'

Ross and Willie looked at each other in confusion.

'That's impossible,' said Willie, knowing only MIT knew about Lianne's identity so far.

Wondering what had spooked them so much, she asked, 'What's the matter? It's like you've both seen a ghost.'

Willie held his phone out to her. 'A police detective came around here asking about this woman? This woman here?' He gave her a chance to change her mind, but he could tell that Margaret was in no doubt.

'That's the woman he asked about,' she said. 'Lianne something, isn't it? And another one. I can't remember her name. He wanted to see the sign-in register.'

'When did he come here?' Ross asked, taking out his notepad.

'Last week.'

Ross stared in dumb disbelief. 'Last *week*?'

Archie said, 'You never told me about that.'

'You were trying to get that woman out of room six.'

Willie asked, 'What did you tell him?'

'Like I say, Archie was busy. So I showed him the register about this one woman. Then he starts asking about this Lianne woman.'

'You should have told me,' snapped Archie.

Margaret protested, 'The guy took a wee look at the register, and then he was gone a few minutes later. I didn't even see him leave.' She looked in appeal to Archie. 'I've got five rooms still to do and it's already eleven. Can I go?'

Willie stepped forward. 'Sorry, Margaret. What was this detective's name?'

She puffed. 'I don't know. DCI Forrest or something. Aye, Bob Forrest.'

Willie's eyes widened. 'Bob *Torrance*?'

An immediate spark of recognition flashed onto Margaret's face. 'That's it,' she snapped. 'Bob Torrance. That's the one.'

Ross said, 'What was he asking about?'

'The same as you two. Did I remember anyone going to her room.' She turned to Archie. 'You weren't around, so I just told him no. I said you would be back in a few minutes, but he bolted. It was weird now that you mention it.'

Willie was already turning towards the main door. 'Thank you. You've both been very helpful.'

Ross didn't understand why they were leaving already, but he didn't want to question his superior in front of Archie and Margaret. Once they were a safe distance outside, Ross asked, 'What's going on? And how the hell was this Bob Torrance digging around about Lianne last week?'

'I don't know the answer to that yet,' said Willie, marching back to the car. 'But there's another problem with all this.'

'Like what?'

'Bob Torrance retired twelve years ago.'

CHAPTER FOURTEEN

Willie and Ross were on the move back to the car.

Willie took out his phone, and called the number at the top of his most popular numbers. When he got an answer, he said, 'John, it's Willie. We've got a problem here.'

Lomond and Donna were en route back to Helen Street, the sound of traffic on the M8 interfering with the call.

'Say that again?' said Lomond.

Willie replied, 'I said, Bob Torrance was at the hostel last week, asking questions about Lianne Gribbin.'

A long pause followed.

'But that's impossible,' said Lomond.

'I know,' Willie replied.

'Almost impossible. What's he playing at? Even putting aside impersonating an officer when he's retired about, what, ten years?'

'Twelve,' Willie corrected him.

'And why was he sniffing around about Lianne a week before her body was found? A retired detective just happens to be enquiring about a twenty-year-old cold case the week before?'

'That's not all,' said Willie.

'Christ, what next?'

'I was talking to Pardeep and Jason before we went in. They had a tail on them this morning. All the way from the station out to the car wash Thomas Rafferty works at.'

'How sure is he?' asked Lomond.

'When Jason tried to pursue him, he sped off. Red flags all over the place.'

'We were in with Brenda Gribbin. Did they put out a description or a registration plate? If they were on the M74, NPR will be able to nail the car down. They might even be able to track them down on the road right now.'

'They didn't get much, other than it was a silver Hyundai. Reg ending NGY.'

There was murmuring on the other end of the phone, making Willie strain to hear what was going on.

'Are you there?' Willie asked.

'Aye,' said Lomond. 'Donna just noticed something.'

'What?'

'We've got a silver Hyundai behind us. Reg ends with NGY.'

Willie immediately broke into a run. 'We're coming to you.'

Lomond appreciated the gesture of loyalty, but couldn't help but chuckle. 'Willie, we're passing the Clyde Tunnel turnoff, we'll be at the station in two minutes. If this guy's dumb enough to try and follow us in there, I'm sure we'll have some guys to help us out.'

Next to Lomond, Donna asked, 'Can't we just take him in?'

Lomond beamed a proud smile. 'Did you hear that, you two? Donna wants us to take him in.' Speaking to Donna now,

Lomond said, 'We're best leaving him in the wind. He might lead us to something useful.' He relayed the full registration, then told Willie to get an ID. 'You know, on second thoughts. I like Donna's plan.'

'John,' Willie began, sounding a note of caution, 'do you really think that's wise?'

'We've got twenty years to catch up on, Willie,' Lomond replied. 'It's time to make something happen.'

'I don't like it, John.'

'Yeah, neither do I, but needs must.' He hung up. Then slowly, Lomond stepped on the accelerator, cruising out into the fast lane. He smiled again when he saw the Hyundai following. He then said to Donna, 'You might want to hold onto something. This isn't exactly recommended in the Police Scotland handbook.'

CHAPTER FIFTEEN

To Donna's surprise, the first thing Lomond did was slow down. He pulled into the slow lane, ceding the middle lane to the driver following them in the Hyundai.

Then Lomond swerved right and floored the accelerator.

Alternating his gaze between the lorry in front, and the Hyundai, Lomond asked, 'Can you get a look at him?'

Donna leaned forward and back, trying to see. 'He's turned his face.'

'Doesn't matter,' said Lomond. 'We'll have him soon.'

The Hyundai sped up further, veering recklessly into the fast lane, only to be blocked by a taxi who wanted to go three miles an hour faster than someone in the middle lane. The Hyundai swerved back into the middle, then shot hard left to undertake, racing into the empty road ahead, and passing the taxi still holding up traffic in the fast lane.

'That's our cue,' said Lomond, flooring the accelerator in pursuit.

Donna gripped her seatbelt tighter. "I thought we were trying to get away from him."

"That's what I hoped he thought as well." Lomond glanced at his left mirror. "Keep an eye on my blind spot, will you? This isn't exactly in the Highway Code."

With no blue lights or sirens, Lomond looked like a regular maniac, weaving through traffic to match the Hyundai's reckless moves. The chase continued past the turnoff for Helen Street police station, which amused Lomond.

"I'll bet he was hoping we would have come off there," he chuckled.

"I know I was," Donna replied, looking longingly at the Govan junction as they raced past.

"Shite," said Lomond as the Hyundai pulled further ahead. "He's got some game." To counter, Lomond swerved across the chevrons marking the Govan slip road where traffic was joining the M8.

Donna, keeping a close eye to her left, slapped the dashboard. "Right, right, right," she called out.

"SHITE!" Lomond shouted, steering hard right to avoid a collision with a Range Rover.

STUCK IN SLOWER, merging traffic, Lomond had only one option. He veered onto the hard shoulder, gaining on the Hyundai until Donna noticed a problem.

"JOHN, YOU SEE THAT, RIGHT?"

"YEP," he said through gritted teeth.

The barrier was narrowing the hard shoulder ahead, leaving them with nowhere to go. Lomond had to scrape against the barrier, using every inch of the hard shoulder. The crunch of metal alerted a motorbike, which took evasive action, preventing a collision that could have stopped them abruptly.

SOMEHOW, they emerged ahead of the congestion. The motorway was clearer, but it was unclear which way the Hyundai would go. It weaved between the left lanes for the M74 and M77 and the right lanes for the M8 Edinburgh.

"WATCH HIM HERE," Donna said, still catching her breath.

"If he's smart, he'll go left. Kingston Bridge will be solid at this time of day," Lomond replied.

When the Hyundai sharply cut left towards the M74, Lomond triumphantly hit the steering wheel with the heel of his hand. "I know where he's going," he announced.

As the road expanded from two lanes to four in a chaotic stretch of motorway, traffic merged from both sides, and slowed to a crawl. But not the Hyundai, nor Lomond.

The Hyundai remained in the lane for the M74 for Carlisle, but Lomond slowed and slotted into the far-left lane, readying for the turnoff to Scotland Street and Shields Road. For a moment, the Hyundai thought that Lomond was gone.

"What are you doing?" asked Donna. "You've done all that, and now you're letting him get away?"

"He's not going on the M74. He knows he'll never get away on that. It's too open. He needs to get off the motorway now."

To Donna's surprise, Lomond was right. Just before the Kinning Park exit, the Hyundai violently turned left, cutting into the slip road. It was only three cars ahead of Lomond now, who had a plan to close the gap to zero.

"Okay," he told Donna. "This is the part that's not really in the Highway Code..."

"Oh shit," she muttered.

It wasn't so much a roundabout under the motorway flyover as an oblong, separated by huge pillars holding up the flyover, and a raised kerb with an empty pavement in the middle.

The Hyundai tore ahead, screeching around the hard right corner, the driver already preparing for the ninety-degree left turn onto Scotland Street. But he never made it that far. He had to slam on his brakes as Lomond's car suddenly appeared ahead, spearing straight towards him.

Lomond had cut the roundabout in half by mounting the kerb, blasting over it, and then turning to take the roundabout in the wrong direction. With nowhere to go, the Hyundai driver relented and stopped. Horns blared all around as no one realized that Lomond and Donna were on police business.

The driver made no attempt to escape. He knew it was over.

Donna and Lomond charged out of the car. In moments like this, a Police Scotland detective can feel very vulnerable, with no weapons at their disposal other than a terse tone of voice.

Lomond prowled towards the Hyundai, expecting the driver to make one last attempt to escape now that they had left their car. Instead, the driver raised his hands inside the car and gestured that he was willing to get out.

Donna stood close to Lomond, ready to pounce if anything untoward happened. As the man got out of the driver's side, Lomond squinted.

"Bob?" he said in amazement.

The driver replied meekly, "Long time no see, John."

As car horns continued to blast around them, with traffic at the roundabout coming to a standstill, Donna asked, "What's going on? Who is he?"

"Donna," said Lomond. "Meet DCI Bob Torrance. Or should I say former DCI Bob Torrance."

'Not quite,' said Torrance. 'I'm with Serious Crime Review, John.' He did a quick scan of the traffic chaos surrounding them. 'We should go somewhere and talk. It's not safe here. And I don't just mean the traffic.'

CHAPTER SIXTEEN

PARDEEP, Jason, Ross, and Willie's phones all pinged with the same message from Lomond:

"*MEET ME AT 12 HOLLOWAY VALLEY ROAD, BEARSDEN. NOW. NO EXCUSES.*"

Followed by a thumbs-up emoji.

IN THE CAR after setting the sat-nav for the address, Willie asked, 'How much do you know about Torrance?'

'Not much,' admitted Ross. 'But I heard a few whispers.'

'Like what?'

Ross shrugged. 'I don't know, it's probably nothing...but kind of weird stuff. That he was into swinging.'

'I'm begging you not to tell me how you would know a thing like that.'

'It's Police Scotland, Willie. All we've got to talk about are cases and each other's private lives.'

'Christ,' Willie puffed, 'I dread to think what'll be said about me once I've packed it in.'

'Did the gaffer work with him?'

'Aye, both of us did. He was our SIO on a couple of big ones. He never quite broke through. I was about to say Dalmarnock, but it was Pitt Street back then. They didn't like Bob much. They thought he was hard work.'

'What was he like?'

Willie paused to think about it. 'A bit like John. But more serious. Could be a bit obsessive. I think he struggled to let go of cold cases. Guys like him, the job just takes them over.'

Ross leaned slightly towards him. 'I think you mean the job takes *over* them.'

Willie shook his head. 'Very clever. Was there a special column about grammar in one of your men's fashion magazines I saw lying on your desk the other day?'

Ross's cheery demeanour vanished. 'It's not about fashion, it's a style magazine. It encompasses a variety of...oh, why am I bothering? I'm talking to a guy who shaves his own hair and his wife buys his clothes.'

'You should try it, sunshine. Maybe your bird will find you some trousers that actually go past your ankles.'

'They're called cut-offs, actually. They're not a mistake. They're a conscious choice.'

Willie sucked his lips in to keep from laughing. 'Whatever you say, Ross.'

IN PARDEEP'S CAR, the atmosphere was a good deal more cordial.

Still on an adrenaline high after his brief chase with the

silver saloon, Jason had no idea that they were being directed to the driver's house. Their conversation was more focussed on what Thomas Rafferty had said.

'What do you reckon, then?' Jason asked, always interested in Pardeep's instincts.

He shook his head. 'He didn't do it. I don't care what his record says. The man we spoke to there never killed Lianne Gribbin.'

'It was twenty years ago, though. He could have been a completely different guy.'

'I think the boss is right,' said Pardeep. 'It doesn't fit. Rafferty could barely string a sentence together. You think he's the kind to be attaching horse bridles to his girlfriend, digging a grave by the River Clyde, and getting away with it for two decades? If you ask me, his wheel's spinning but the hamster's dead.'

'Huge proportion of murders are carried out by people known to the victim. The stats bear that out.'

'I don't care what the stats say,' Pardeep said. 'I think the key's this older guy that Lianne was seeing. That's a dimension to the enquiry no one knew about when she went missing. There's basic chains of evidence that have been missed. A hidden relationship with an unknown older male? How can that just be coming to light now?'

'It was Strathclyde Police days,' said Jason. 'From what I've read on the subject, it was the wild, wild west around here.'

'Jason, mate, you've no idea. The stories I've heard over the years...I don't know why, but I feel like we're wandering into one of those stories as we speak.'

'What the hell,' said Jason, as they pulled up outside Bob Torrance's house in the middle of a sedate but sprawling hillside of bungalows in Bearsden, just off the ever-busy Switchback Road.

In the driveway, was the silver saloon Hyundai that had tormented part of Jason's morning.

When he and Pardeep knocked on the front door, it was opened by Bob Torrance.

'I believe I owe you an apology,' said Torrance.

In the living room behind him, Lomond was on the couch drinking a cup of coffee, examining old enquiry files with Donna. Noticing Jason and Pardeep lingering on the doorstep, Lomond called out, 'Come in, boys. It's fine.'

Once the whole team had convened in Torrance's living room, he stood in front of the fireplace, ready to give a talk he had been preparing for a long time now, but had no one to share it with.

As Torrance had explained earlier, his wife Elaine was up the stairs, bed-ridden from a traumatic brain injury years earlier. Although incapable of speech or walking, she had retained most of her motor function from the waist up. Like a hospital bed, she had a call button attached to the bed frame if she ever needed anything – though Torrance was in the habit of checking on her every fifteen minutes while at home. When he was out working, a carer would come in to check on her, but it severely limited Torrance's ability to work. Hence the state of the living room, which looked like someone had been hoarding office paperwork.

With Elaine incapacitated, Bob had allowed work to completely take over downstairs. Work life had invaded the home like an infestation of bamboo, its roots breaking through from the ground up, swallowing up everything in sight.

There were boxes piled high against every wall, as if he was moving house. If the MIT officers looked closely, they could still see some evidence of what had once been a living room, but over time the scope of Torrance's work had taken over every facet of the room. The TV in the corner had become a board for sticky notes. Piles of framed photos that had once adorned the walls now sat in stacks leaning against the skirting board, taken down to make way for the dozens upon dozens of photocopied enquiry files, notes, maps, witness and suspect photos that were now stuck on the wall. Lomond couldn't help but be reminded of what his own living room in his old flat in Paisley had once looked like, dedicated to his search for the Sandman. But what Torrance had put together over the years put that in the shade. Clearly, whatever Torrance had been working on was more than sheer dedication or even obsession. It had taken over his entire life – and his home.

When Lomond had enquired as to whether Torrance had permission to be in possession of all the case file boxes, Torrance gave no answer other than to say they were just copies. Unofficial copies.

He drew his hands together and began. 'You're probably all wondering what you're doing here. And, apart from John, be wondering who the hell I am. My name's Bob Torrance, I'm a retired former Detective Chief Inspector who spent his final years in Glasgow Central. Before that, Cathcart and East Ren, so I was about a fair bit. I was John's SIO for a couple of years.' He then said to Lomond, 'That was over at Pitt Street before they pulled the shit hole down.'

Lomond smiled and nodded.

Torrance continued, 'And then a few years in Paisley. I retired a while back. Twelve years, in fact. But I've asked you all to be here for me to talk to you about some of my findings as part of the Serious Crime Review Unit.'

Pardeep snorted, then looked to the ceiling. 'Of course. I should have known.'

'Maybe I speak for myself,' ventured Jason, 'but what is that?'

Lomond was about to answer, but deferred to Torrance.

He explained, 'The SCRU is a specialised team within Police Scotland who are dedicated solely to re-investigating unsolved crimes. These are typically high-profile cases. Your murder enquiries that make it into the papers or on the telly. But the unit's focus is exclusively on cold cases. The ones that have just been left behind.'

'I'm sorry,' said Donna. 'But I thought you were retired.'

Lomond, Willie, and Pardeep already knew the reason for this apparent anomaly.

'Part of the SCRU's methodology,' explained Torrance, 'is employing former detectives who have specialised in certain fields to work on enquiries. We review cold cases, looking for new or overlooked evidence that sometimes a pair of fresh eyes can help with. As well as bringing fresh blood and greater experience onto a case, where sometimes that wasn't the case.'

'If it's Serious Crime Review,' said Pardeep, 'then why have you been digging around about Lianne Gribbin? She was a prostitute who went missing twenty years ago.' Announcing to his colleagues, 'Did you know that he was sniffing around Copeland House last week, the hostel Lianne was living in? Do you want to explain to DCI Lomond why you were doing that? Because that strikes me as highly unusual, a week before her remains are found.'

Torrance smiled at Pardeep, holding his unwavering gaze. He then turned to Lomond. 'You've got good ones here, John. I must say I'm a bit jealous. It's like you're a football manager but the board gave you all the players you wanted to buy. I was too often left to manage Second and Third Division players. But you...you've got proper Premiership stars here. I can tell.'

Not about to let him off the hook, Pardeep's stare intensified. 'Could you answer the question, please, Mr Torrance?'

Lomond knew what Pardeep was doing by calling him that. A subtle reminder that he might be involved with SCRU, but there was only one person in the room no longer officially police personnel. A regular citizen officially. And that was Bob Torrance.

He said to Pardeep, 'I promise you I can explain. But you're coming at this all backwards. I didn't go to Copeland House solely because of Lianne Gribbin. She was just part of the reason I was there.' He shook his head and looked down at his feet. 'If you only knew what you've stumbled onto...'

Uncharacteristically quiet so far, Lomond finally spoke. 'Why don't you tell us, Bob?'

The answer was something that Torrance had wanted to share for a long time with someone in a position to do something about it. But he knew the reaction he would get. He had lived with the evidence for a while now. He'd had time to make peace with the facts and settled on his conclusions. At first blush, it sounded outlandish.

More than that, in fact.

What Torrance had to say could scarcely be believed.

CHAPTER SEVENTEEN

TORRANCE DECIDED that the best way to explain, was to jump straight to the end of his conclusions. He cleared his throat, tense with apprehension and anticipation. 'There's a list somewhere with the names of every High Court judge, senior legal official, and senior police figure who has used prostitutes, and in some cases groomed minors to commit sexual acts.'

Ross pursed his lips, then lifted his hands up to drop them theatrically onto his thighs with a slap. 'Oh okay. So it's tinfoil hat time...'

Pardeep, Jason, and Donna all made similar noises of discontent. The only one whose body language was in poker mode was Lomond.

Ross got up as if to leave.

Lomond said, 'Ross, sit down.' Internally, his reaction wasn't far off Ross's, but he at least wanted to hear Torrance out.

Ross paused, then sat back down again. For the moment, his credulity – along with the others' – was still firmly intact. But he was at least prepared now to hear Torrance out.

'I know a lot of stuff has gone around about me over the years,' Torrance began, taking a seat on an overflowing file box. He leaned forward on his knees. 'I can assure you none of it's true. The truth is that I've never really fit in anywhere. Not in police college, and certainly not in the force itself. Some people might call me odd. Maybe a bit of an eccentric. And that's fine. I've always been a bit of a loner. It makes me a good investigator, but probably not a great Detective Chief Inspector. I didn't join the police to make friends. I've never really *had* friends. Haven't had much use for them, to be honest. That makes someone like me an easy target for rumours and gossip. I've never tried very hard to correct any of the things said about me. I just got on with the job. Maybe that's why I got the shout for the Serious Crime Review Unit. Being a bit of an obsessive...' He gestured at their surroundings. 'And I know what this room makes me look like. But someone like me is a good fit for somewhere like SCRU. You get on with the job. Work on your own mostly, then submit your findings.' He addressed Pardeep. 'To answer your answer DC Varma, what was I doing asking about Lianne Gribbin a week before her body was found? Well, you made the first mistake that investigators are prone to. You made an assumption.'

Pardeep widened his eyes at the accusation.

Torrance continued, 'You assumed that I only started looking for Lianne last week. When in actual fact, I've been looking for her for the last ten years.' He turned to Lomond. 'It was after our time together, John, but Lianne Gribbin was given to me at Pitt Street CID. After your team moved on from it, I kept at it. Then I lobbied for it to be picked up again at Serious Crime Review after I retired. They brought me back on, but it was shut down again. Just as I was making progress. I've been working it myself ever since.'

'What brought you to Copeland House then?' asked Pardeep.

'Someone that none of you will have heard of yet. And with good reason. But to explain that, I need to go back to the beginning. You see, all this started with a missing girl back in the late nineties. How many of you are familiar with Boland Castle Hospital?'

Only Lomond and Willie acknowledged that they were.

Torrance said, 'Well, for the rest of you, Boland Castle was an institution for people with learning difficulties. You'd never even know it was there now. It's out by Strathblane Road and the way out to the Campsies. It spread out over dozens of acres, and was made up of about ten different blocks all built around the ruins of the old castle. At its height, there were over a thousand people kept there. There was even a home for the nurses on site. When it opened in the thirties, it was regarded as one of the most advanced care facilities in the country. But by the eighties, all that had changed. Funding had ebbed away to such an extent that reports showed many patients were malnourished or mistreated. Something about being hidden away in the woods at the foot of the Campsies gave certain carers a notion that they could get away with whatever they wanted. Patients were routinely abused or beaten. Made to sleep on cold floor tiles without any bedding. Toilets restricted for entire days. Over the years, inspectors tried to sound the alarm over what was happening, but they weren't seeing the worst of it. All this stuff only started to come out when a nurse made a complaint to Strathclyde Police about one of the carers. The carer was charged with assault, and the trial was...well, a shit show. You need to understand the state of social care at that time in the nineties. The mentality was still very much that people with learning difficulties or disabilities were just shut away somewhere. They weren't cared for, they were just housed. Gradually, care in the community became more of a thing, giving patients their lives back instead of treating them like prisoners. The outrage of it all was that so many of the so-called patients there had absolutely nothing medically wrong with them, or any special need. Back then, if there was anything about your kid you didn't understand, or they were a bit unruly, it wasn't that hard to ship them off somewhere like Boland Castle. There were a lot of kids there that didn't have anything wrong with them, per se. They were from disadvantaged backgrounds. Maybe a bit wild. Boland Castle was like somewhere in between a borstal and a hospital. Somewhere to just send unwanted kids away to. With no family or friends coming to see them, they had no way of knowing how or if they would ever get out. One of those kids was a girl called Angela Devlin.'

Willie's brow furrowed. 'I remember that name.'

'Then you're one of the few who do,' Torrance replied.

Willie turned to Lomond. 'The trial that collapsed.'

Suddenly remembering, Lomond said, 'Oh aye...'

Feeling helplessly out of the loop, Ross said, 'What trial?'

Realising he'd jumped ahead, Torrance said, 'Sorry. So what happened, right...Angela Devlin ran away from Boland Castle. Escaped out her ward in the middle of the night. Somehow, without any money, she managed to get herself all the way to Edinburgh. There was a huge manhunt at the time, and I spearheaded it. It took two weeks, but someone recognised her walking around drunk and high on drugs on Princes Street. When Edinburgh police took her in, and once they'd sobered her up, they asked her where she had been staying. She said she didn't know what it was called, but she could take them there. At this stage, I came through, and along with the local DI there, we took a car to where Angela said she was staying. Or as she put it, she'd been taken. Turns out, she'd been picked up around Glasgow city centre the night she'd run away, and plied with booze and drugs. Bear in mind, this was a young girl who'd never had a drink in her life before. She was taken to this flat in Edinburgh's New Town, where she was kept intoxicated and drugged, and forced to have sex with a number of adult men over the course of the next fourteen days. The case against the men using the property was airtight. Their defence had been that she'd told them she was eighteen, and that not only had she been a willing participant of this abuse, she had asked to be paid. The only problem with their defence was that Angela Devlin wasn't the only minor to have been found in the property. When Edinburgh police raided the flat, they found two young boys and a girl, none of whom were older than fourteen years old.'

Lomond was surprised at what he was hearing. 'A child abuse den in the middle of Edinburgh?'

'That's what we all thought,' said Torrance. 'The whole thing was so brazen. And the entire time, the suspects acted like they'd done nothing wrong, and it was all a big misunderstanding. At no point did they ever seem worried. Like they knew nothing would ever come of the charges. But the charges didn't go away. And the Crown Office agreed with me and my report that there was a case to answer, and so a trial date was set.' He took a deep breath then let out a long puff. 'That's when everything went to hell in a handcart.'

CHAPTER EIGHTEEN

'What happened?' asked Lomond.

'First of all, let's be clear about the scale of the charges. It was dozens of charges brought against five men, in a whole range of crimes committed at that property against minors. All of them runaways or missing. At sixteen, Angela Devlin was the oldest victim. The case against the men – as I say – was airtight. And on top of that, we had probably the best silk in the country prosecuting for us.'

'Silk?' said Jason.

Lomond explained, 'A QC. Or a KC now, I guess. It's because of the silk gowns they wear.'

Torrance continued, 'As the Crown Prosecution Service instructs QCs or KCs to act either on the behalf of the defence or prosecution on complex or high-profile cases, being merely excellent at your job isn't enough. It's highly political. A lot of backroom meetings required. A real establishment figure. But sometimes a rogue gets through the system. And we had the biggest rogue of them all on our side. We had Bruce Murdock.'

'Who's Bruce Murdock?' asked Donna.

Torrance trilled his lips as he let out a long exhalation. 'How best to describe Bruce Murdock...Larger than life? Literally as well as figuratively. He's a very big guy. Grossly overweight. Has this strange walk, almost like a penguin. Sort of leans back and can barely swing his arms. A big personality.'

Lomond said, 'He retired, I thought?'

'Yeah, a while ago,' Torrance replied. 'Back in the day, he was a real storyteller too. You could sit with him for hours just listening to him, and it felt like five minutes. The sort of guy who doesn't just talk to you. He holds court. You know what I mean?'

'A real *bon viveur*,' Lomond added, remembering impressions of him from news clips and photos of him that appeared around some of the biggest cases in Scottish legal history. He then asked Willie, 'Always walked around with a cane, didn't he?'

Willie nodded. 'Aye. Bit weird, if you ask me.'

'Wore this fedora everywhere he went. Tartan trousers. A real throwback. He looked like something out of the thirties.'

'Aye,' Willie said again. 'Bit weird.'

Lomond smiled to himself. He knew that to Willie, anything outside of a dark grey suit from Next for work, or jeans and a t-shirt at the weekend was deemed a 'bit weird' for a man to be wearing.

Torrance continued, 'The problems began before the trial even started. In the weeks leading up to the start date, rumours started circulating around the Edinburgh legal scene that Angela Devlin was going to testify that the trial judge had been one of the many men who had visited the flat to pay for sex with her.'

Suddenly, it felt like all the oxygen in the room had evaporated. Everyone was stunned.

'Are you serious?' said Lomond.

Now on the edge of his seat, Pardeep asked, 'Was it true?'

Donna, Ross, and Jason waded in too.

'Where did the rumour come from?'

'What did Angela Devlin say about it?'

'How did I never hear about this?'

Torrance gestured for them all to slow down. 'I asked all of these questions at the time and never got answers. Angela Devlin disappeared from her temporary accommodation. But the rumour about the trial judge appeared to have legs, though. Because I got word that the advocate depute – the prosecutor for the crown – had suddenly accepted plea deals for ninety-nine per cent of the charges. Most of the men pled guilty to reduced charges and walked free. No jail time. Only one man was given a prison sentence, and even that was suspended.'

Lomond said, 'You must have been climbing the walls.'

Torrance scoffed. 'I didn't understand how it could happen. Plea deals happen all the time before trials.' He gestured towards Lomond and Willie. 'You guys know that. But plea deals to this extent? Never in all my days.'

Lomond asked, 'Did you ever find out if the rumour was true?'

'I never saw any evidence of it. But Murdock told me that something highly suspect must have happened behind the scenes. When I pressed my superiors to find out what exactly had happened, they told me that the CPS had told them that it wasn't in the public interest to pursue such damaging testimony involving a long trial that could prove painful for the witnesses if forced to relive the abuse they had suffered.'

Ross exclaimed, 'They actually used the scale of the abuse to shut the trial down?' He scoffed, then looked around the room, wondering how such a thing could happen. 'The abuse against the victims was so bad, it was better to let the defendants *get away* with it?'

He wasn't the only one outraged.

Torrance shrugged. 'I understand your anger, believe me. I've lived with that outrage for years.'

Donna asked, 'What about Angela Devlin?'

Torrance replied, 'She was found a month later in a heroin den in Falkirk. She retracted all cooperation with any further investigations, and refused to answer any questions about the trial judge rumours.'

He walked over to a stack of boxes that appeared to be in complete disarray. Carefully, he lifted the lid of the second box down, extracting a stack of files held together with an elastic band. 'Six months later, she was dead of an overdose. Speaking of which...' He removed the elastic band, rifling through the various files, holding each one aloft as he reached a conclusion. 'Other victims from the Edinburgh flat. Suicide. Suicide. Overdose. Suicide. Unexplained death. Death ruled inconclusive. Murdered, perpetrator never caught. Murdered, perpetrator never caught again.' He re-banded the files and returned them to their exact place.

Lomond was certain that Torrance could have told him where a specific file was in any of the boxes, he was so entrenched with the material.

Torrance finished by saying, 'All of those deaths came within two years of the trial collapsing. Six months after the trial collapsed, the judge, Lord Baker Windermere, quietly retired then disappeared off to the south of France. He died of a heart attack a few months later.'

Looking out the tops of his eyes, Ross glanced worriedly towards Lomond, trying to gauge his reaction to what they had just been told.

Lomond took a long intake of breath. 'Are you saying you think Lord Windermere was murdered? That all these people were bumped off to cover up a conspiracy?'

'I'm not saying anything,' Torrance retorted. 'These are just the facts of what's happened since that trial. I wrote a report detailing my concerns about obstruction of justice. I mean, we're talking about a sitting judge being implicated in the very crimes that he was supposed to be sitting in judgement on. Not *only* that, but it appeared that senior figures in the Scottish legal establishment had helped to protect him from any accusations ever being made public. I knew what would happen as soon as I handed my report in. Of course it was buried and hidden in a drawer somewhere. It was probably buried with the rubble of the old Pitt Street headquarters when they tore it down. I kept making enough noise about it to force an enquiry, but that was whitewashed. My report was dismissed. Soon after I was sidelined, relegated to minor cases. It was a way of forcing me out. With Elaine to look after, I decided to call it a day. I retired soon after.'

In the silence that followed, everyone in the room needed a minute to organise their thoughts. Torrance had just launched decades of conspiracy, innuendo, and hard facts at them. What he expected them to do with the information now was unclear.

'It's a hell of a story, Bob,' Lomond offered. 'But what does any of it have to do with Lianne Gribbin?'

Jason emphasised, 'And why you've been following all of us around this morning?'

Torrance replied, 'I had to find out who else was looking into Lianne Gribbin's disappearance. I didn't want it botched a second time. Not on my watch.'

Lomond asked, 'Are you suggesting there are elements in the police who don't want this solved?'

Torrance hesitated. 'I don't want to answer that. Not yet. But I *will* say this. I went to the Copeland hostel trying to find someone. You see, when I came out of retirement to help with the Serious Crime Review Unit, I found a cold case that no one else wanted to touch. A murder enquiry. The victim was a woman called Tricia Dunn who was found strangled six years ago, her body dumped behind an advertising hoarding in Trongate. She'd stayed for a while at Copeland House. And just like Angela Devlin years earlier, she'd been a patient at...' He trailed off on purpose.

Lomond said, 'Boland Castle hospital.'

'Exactly right,' Torrance replied.

Ross, in a rush to follow up, said, 'The manager told Willie and I that you were over there last week. But you weren't asking questions about Tricia Dunn. You were asking about Lianne Gribbin. Why?'

Torrance shook his head like it was all a misunderstanding. 'I went there last week to look for any paperwork relating to Tricia Dunn's stay. The guy Archie there runs a tight ship, because he pulled out sign-in registers for every day she'd stayed there. But given that I've been on the Lianne Gribbin enquiry from day one, I asked about her as well. I spoke to the cleaner, and she let me look at the registers. That's when I noticed a familiar name. A visitor that had come to see Tricia Dunn numerous times.' Torrance looked in Ross's direction. 'You must know by now what joins the dots between Lianne Gribbin and Tricia Dunn.'

Ross squinted in confusion as the penny dropped. 'Surely not.'

'Oh yes,' replied Torrance. 'Walter Murdock. He visited Tricia Dunn eight times in the weeks running up to her death.' He walked across the room towards an evidence photo pinned to the wall. On his way, he said, 'Six detectives in the room. Not one of you noticed this.'

'To be fair,' said Willie, 'it's pretty chokka in here, Bob.'

Torrance took down the evidence photo and handed it to Lomond without a word.

Lomond stared at it for several seconds. Then looked up at Torrance.

'Makes sense now?' asked Torrance.

Lomond handed the photo to Willie, but no one else could see what it was yet.

'What is it?' Ross asked.

The moment the photo was out of Lomond's hand, he walked towards the living room window and shook his head.

It was now Willie's turn to stare in incomprehension at the photo. 'Fuckin' hell,' he said quietly to himself.

Ross came over demanding to see it, then had the same reaction to it as Lomond and Willie. He held it up for the others to see.

Lomond checked, 'That's what I think it is, right?'

Torrance wasn't happy about the answer he had to give. 'Yep,' he said.

Pardeep, Jason, and Donna all crowded around to see the photo.

It showed a woman lying on her back, clothes partly ripped from her body. Her eyes were open, but her body was lifeless. Pale, having lain undiscovered for several hours before the alarm was raised.

Torrance said, 'That's Tricia Dunn.'

In her mouth was a metal bit, the kind that goes in a horse's mouth – a metal bar with a ring on each end for attaching to a horse's bridle.

Torrance explained, 'Lianne Gribbin might not have been the first. But she was certainly not the last.'

Putting everyone's movements that morning into place in his head, Lomond ventured, 'You found out about Lianne this morning, didn't you?'

Torrance replied, 'Moira and I go back a fair bit. I asked her to tell me if anything else like Tricia Dunn ever came up.'

'What made you think something would?'

'There's lots more where Tricia Dunn and Lianne Gribbin came from. Don't you get it? They're just the start of something terrifying.'

Everyone's heads were still spinning from the revelation.

Torrance concluded, 'I think whoever killed Lianne Gribbin didn't stop there. I think he's out there still.'

Given what he'd just seen, Lomond had no choice but to agree. 'And if that's the case, it might only be a matter of time before he strikes again.'

CHAPTER NINETEEN

At first glance, they appeared to be two regular men in their late fifties walking down the street. Wearing perhaps not very trendy clothes. The younger of the two, Barry, wore slightly baggy, unflattering jeans, hanging down a bit at the back. Along with a polo shirt, and a jacket that was one size too big for him and too warm for the late-spring weather. His brother Peter looked like he had shopped at Marks and Spencer, rather than Barry's Primark efforts.

The differences between the men became more apparent as time went on. Like the fact that neither man was talking to the other. And, often, the men didn't even walk together. Peter walked a few steps ahead of Barry, normally carrying some food shopping bags. Peter would be focussed on the path ahead, while Barry had his head bowed, not burdened by any bags. But certainly not unburdened.

The walk had become a ritual – since Barry's release. Every Monday, Peter arrived at ten a.m. sharp at Barry's tenement flat in Govan. Then they would do the five-minute walk to Farmfoods at Govan Cross. Peter would carry the basket for Barry.

Nothing that happened there was ever a surprise. Barry bought the same things every week, in the same quantities. All from the same microwaveable range. Macaroni and cheese. Cottage pie. Chicken chow mein. It was all about routine.

Barry had become used to routine.

Routine was what had made passing the time inside passable. Each moment was just a countdown to the next event. Wake-up. Showers. Breakfast. Leisure time. Rehab. Psychological evaluation. On and on it went, for each day of his sentence.

Now that he was back out in the real world, Barry craved routine more than ever. Without it, his life fell apart.

The men went round the shop in near-silence. The only utterances between them occurred if Peter wanted to check if the price of something was okay, or if Barry wanted a different quantity. But Barry always wanted the same.

Peter preferred to keep a distance. Not just because it was easier for him to not have to talk to his brother. It was also safer.

After the trial, life hadn't been easy for Peter either. Once Barry's identity had been revealed by the press, suddenly strangers in the street had plenty to say to Peter.

'Creep,' was a typical one. Also 'weirdo'.

Then there were the ones who simply spat at him.

What Barry had done was enough for Peter to resent him already. But now that Barry was out of prison, Peter only felt two emotions walking the streets with him: contempt and shame.

It was Tuesday. Which meant a stop off at the bookies on the way home. Peter had no time for such places. He couldn't fathom the punters' willingness to throw money away with such little prospect of reward. Though winnings weren't the real reason for Barry's visit. It never was.

Nobody noticed the two brothers enter the bookies. They

couldn't have been more anonymous as people. Peter stood holding the carrier bags, counting down the time until they could go.

Barry stood a few paces away, watching the TV screens as horses were paraded around the pre-race paddock. His mouth hung open a little bit. His eyes glazed like someone in terrible need of sleep.

This was the part that always made Peter uncomfortable. The way Barry stared at the horses. Sometimes Barry mouthed things to himself. Peter never got close enough to hear, but he wasn't sure that he wanted to anyway.

Barry scratched his face, then looked around awkwardly, checking that no one was looking. Peter was looking, but Barry didn't care about that. Barry reached down towards his groin, and gave himself a good hard feel.

Peter couldn't stand it. He turned on his heels. 'I'll be outside,' he said.

Barry didn't acknowledge him in any way. He just kept staring at the TV. A little louder this time, he said to himself, 'So beautiful...'

Peter waited for him outside, pacing around with the shopping bags. 'Done then?'

Barry didn't answer.

Peter led the way, staying a few steps in front again.

Everywhere Barry looked, there seemed to be beautiful women. Older women. Younger women. He had never understood how other men discriminated. Fat or thin, tall or short, it didn't matter to Barry. It wasn't about physicality to him. It was about longing. He was still a virgin, and he knew at this point in his life, he was going to die one too. Once he had accepted the fact, it made life more bearable. It made it easier to shield himself from the pain of his loneliness. He had felt lonely since he was a small boy. In prison, psychologically, he had been an open book to even the most junior therapist. Typical textbook stuff. Daddy didn't love me enough, mummy loved me too much.

Now, the way Barry saw it, it made life easier if he just stopped looking. Stopped paying attention to women in the street. That way, his heart couldn't grieve over what he couldn't see. He'd rather die than make eye contact with a stranger, let alone smile at someone.

Back at the flat, Peter had put the Farmfoods shopping away, fitting the same packages into the same spots in the freezer as the previous week. Then, picking up some laundry that had accumulated on the dining table, Peter took it towards Barry's bedroom.

When Barry saw this happen, he launched himself towards the door, grabbing for the handle to keep it shut. 'No,' he cried out. After a long pause, he said, 'It's too messy.'

Peter considered bursting past to get a look, fascinated by what a man who had exposed himself to women could possibly be ashamed of.

Barry took the clothes from Peter's hands then dropped them on the dirty carpet. 'I'll get them later,' Barry told him.

Relieved to have an excuse to go, Peter let him have the clothes. 'Fine,' he said, heading for the door. Then he pointed out a cardboard box that had been left on the doorstep. When he handed it over, Barry snatched it out of his hand.

'See you tomorrow?' asked Peter.

'Yeah,' Barry replied, cradling the cardboard box like there was gold inside. He watched Peter from the living room window. Once he was satisfied that Peter had gone, Barry opened the box in the hall.

His breathing was heavy. His mouth hanging open in anticipation.

The box was marked with the branding from an equestrian website.

Barry tore it open like a child at Christmas. Then he took out the prized item inside.

A brand new metal bit, and a leather bridle.

He took them carefully out of the packaging, the way someone would handle an item they planned on returning and had to keep pristine.

But Barry wouldn't be returning either the bit or the bridle. He had plans for both of them.

He took them to his bedroom.

Inside, the curtains were closed. They had been closed since the day Barry arrived there. He didn't care much for daylight. Or the outside world.

The air was thick with a musty odour, a complete lack of airflow, and stale dirty clothes.

He had the bit and bridle in one hand, and with his free hand opened a cupboard door where a woman was sitting curled up on the floor, surrounded by filthy clothes. She was blindfolded and gagged, but Barry could easily make out her sobs. She had long since given up trying to make her screams heard.

Barry crouched down, and stroked her head. 'It's all right,' he explained. 'It will all be over soon.'

CHAPTER TWENTY

THE MAJOR INVESTIGATIONS team returned to Helen Street for a debriefing on Bob Torrance's findings. DSU Boyle, waiting expectantly in the bullpen, held her arms out when she realised Torrance wasn't with them.

'Where is he?'

Lomond had stormed ahead of the rest of the team. He steamed straight past Linda, telling her, 'Reception's getting him a temporary pass. He doesn't have clearance for MIT.'

She turned, following his direction towards the whiteboard. 'So where are we?' she asked, arms folding tightly.

Lomond picked up a black marker and wrote in large letters in the centre of the board.

"WALTER MURDOCK"

Then he drew three lines that branched out from the name. Before everyone had made it to their desks, Lomond tapped on the name, then told Linda, 'Lianne Gribbin had been staying at the Copeland hostel. While there, she was visited several times by Murdock. The lead was never followed up properly. Bob's got evidence linking Murdock to another murder enquiry. A cold case out of Serious Crime Review.'

Linda shook her head. 'What do we know about Murdock?'

Lomond lifted his eyebrows. 'Ross?' he said sternly, and with increased volume. 'This is the part where you sit up and take a sip of coffee, son.'

Ross put his phone down and snapped to attention. 'Yes, sir,' he began, then said to Linda, 'Ma'am, it appears that Walter Murdock is the son of Bruce Murdock.'

Linda's eyes widened. 'Bruce Murdock, QC?'

Lomond corrected her while writing other notes on the board. 'KC now.'

She shook her head in irritation. 'KC, then. So what's all that about? What's the son of a King's Counsel doing visiting a prostitute in a hostel?'

'Multiple times, too,' Willie added.

Lomond put the lid back on the pen, then turned around to address the team and Linda. 'The answer to that is surely further down the road. For now,' he pointed to what he had just written, 'this is the way forward.'

Against each line branching out from Murdock's name, he had written:

"ANGELA DEVLIN"

"TRICIA DUNN"

"LIANNE GRIBBIN"

Linda gestured with confusion at the board. 'Who are the other two?'

Lomond took them each in turn. 'Angela Devlin. Teen runaway who had been a patient at Boland Castle hospital. Ends up groomed and drugged in a flat in Edinburgh. A rumour spreads that the judge presiding over the case might be called not only as a witness but as a defendant. The trial collapses soon after, and Angela dies quietly of a drug overdose soon after. The counsel assigned to her was Bruce Murdock.' He pointed to the next name. 'Then we have Tricia Dunn. If her juvenile record is anything to go by, she was a handful. She was a patient at Boland as well. But she made it to eighteen and managed to get out. Then she started working as a prostitute around central Glasgow. Appeared to be popular with the other women, and I believe came over here a few times with the Beware Book to pass on concerns about a few punters. Nothing came of those.' He pointed to Pardeep. 'But Pardeep, you can look into that.' Lomond took out a photo of the Tricia Dunn crime scene and stuck it to the whiteboard. 'Six years ago, Tricia Dunn was found here.' He pointed out the bridle around her neck and the bit in her mouth.

Linda peered at the photo, taking a step closer. 'Is that a—'

'Yes, it is,' Lomond replied. 'The same sort of horse-related stuff we found on Lianne Gribbin this morning.'

'You think this is a serial?' asked Linda.

'You don't?' Lomond retorted. He motioned towards the whiteboard as if it was obvious. 'We've got two prostitutes in the centre of Glasgow, both residents in the same hostel, both found dead with horse reins around their heads. How many guys do you think, who are into something like that, are active in this city?'

'I've got no idea,' Linda replied. 'And what do these two have to do with Angela Devlin?'

'The horse bridle and prostitution angle connects Tricia Dunn and Lianne Gribbin, clearly. But not Devlin.'

Donna spoke up, 'In fairness, sir. I get that there's a connection with Boland Castle with Devlin and Dunn. But Devlin wasn't murdered. With the backgrounds of most of the kids who were in Boland Castle, it probably wouldn't be hard to make all sorts of grisly connections between them.'

'True,' Lomond admitted. 'But it all comes down to—'

The office doors swung open, and in stepped former DCI Bob Torrance. 'Murdock,' said Torrance. 'This whole thing is Murdock.'

An appreciative smile appeared on Linda's face. 'Bob Torrance,' she enthused.

'Guv, is it?' he replied.

'We do 'ma'am' these days, Bob. Christ, it was only...how long have you been gone?'

'Twelve years. But I've been back in SCRU the past three.'

'Well, it's good to have a safe pair of hands here.'

Torrance's eyes narrowed as he approached the whiteboard.

Lomond stood aside, yielding to the man he would have comfortably described as his former mentor. 'Do you concur, boss?'

Torrance gave a small smile. 'On Murdock? Sure.'

'It can't be a coincidence that two women who disappear from the same hostel and end up dead in almost identical ways were both visited by him.'

'What about Angela Devlin?' asked Ross.

'What do you mean?' Linda asked.

'She's the outlier here. Wasn't a prostitute, wasn't murdered—'

'We think,' Jason interjected.

Pardeep said, 'Thomas Rafferty told Jason and me that Lianne was being messaged by some guy called Winston or Wilbur or something similar. Surely that must have been Walter?'

'Circumstantial,' Linda told him.

'Not to mention guesswork,' Willie added.

Lomond said, 'A smarter man than me once said, circumstantial doesn't work in court. But it's—'

'Good enough to start an enquiry,' Torrance concluded. He smiled warmly. 'You remembered at least one thing I told you, then.'

'I remembered a damn sight more than that, Bob,' Lomond replied.

Linda had heard enough. 'Bring him in,' she said. 'The Murdock boy. Let's hear what he has to say, at least.' She eyed Pardeep and Jason. 'You two. Bring him in.'

'Ma'am,' they each replied, then set off quickly.

Then she turned to Ross. 'Ross, you too.'

Lomond whipped around from the whiteboard, where he had been making a further note. 'No, Linda. I need him.'

'What for?' she asked.

One thing Lomond was not good at was lying. 'I...just need him here for now.'

Linda didn't want to press him further, though she suspected what the real reason was. She wasn't going to highlight it—and certainly not in front of Lomond's team and his former mentor.

Ross waited for Lomond's instructions.

After a further pause, Lomond said, 'The dead judge in the Angela Devlin case, Lord Windermere. Find out what happened there. Was there any suspicion of foul play in Devlin's death? I want to know what we're facing here.'

'Seriously?' Ross said. 'Surely DCI Torrance can be of more help on that than me?'

Torrance said, 'I'm retired, DS McNair. Just Bob is sufficient.'

Lomond said, 'That's not all. You and Donna track down everything you can on Jimmy Gribbin.'

The pair paused.

Ross said, 'As in...'

'Yes, Lianne's dad,' Lomond answered.

'Why?'

Lomond tutted. 'Because I'm telling you to.'

'I mean, what are we looking for?'

'Well, a written confession detailing how he committed the murders, along with a guarantee that there are no more victims out there.'

Willie said, 'Since when was the dad in the picture?'

'Since this morning,' said Lomond. 'Twenty years ago, there were pictures of Jimmy all over that living room. Along with family photos of holidays and the like. Going back there this morning, it was like Jimmy never existed.' He turned to Linda. 'Remember the day we spoke to Brenda and Jimmy?'

Linda looked blank. 'Not especially.'

'Brenda told us that Lianne changed suddenly in her teens.'

'Wow, fancy that.'

'I'm talking about significant changes in her character. Textbook signs of childhood sexual abuse. Sudden changes in mood or personality. Anxiety. Social withdrawal.'

'Except there's fourteen years between the time of Lianne Gribbin staying at Copeland hostel, and Tricia Dunn staying there. You think Jimmy Gribbin is behind this?'

'I must say, boss,' said Donna, 'it's a bit of a leap based on one picture of a horse in a garden shed.'

Lomond reached into his jacket pocket and produced the photo he'd been hiding there since talking to Brenda Gribbin. 'I want to know everything about the people in that photo. First of all, who are they, and what happened to them? Where was that photo taken, and why did Jimmy hang onto it all these years?'

'Honestly,' said Linda, 'I think you're reaching. A picture of a horse? An old photograph?'

Lomond replied, 'It's not just about a picture of a horse. Or a bridle. It's about an overall pattern of behaviour, and the clear evidence that something broke down between Brenda and Jimmy since Lianne's disappearance.'

'People grow apart, John.'

'Yes, they do,' he replied. 'And they don't go out of their way to not talk about it the way Brenda did. It wasn't just removing someone from the house. It was as if she was pretending he had never existed in the first place.'

'Okay,' said Ross. 'So everything we can find on the Angela Devlin case, and anything on Jimmy Gribbin.'

'And another thing. Archie the hostel manager said he tried to speak to an officer about Walter Murdock but was dismissed. Find out who it was.' Lomond waved Willie over. 'Willie, you're with me and Bob. We're going to talk to Moira, then we're going to find Bruce Murdock.'

'What do you want to talk to him for?' Linda asked.

'The Murdocks are up to their necks in this thing. I want to find out exactly what happened with Angela Devlin.'

As Ross and Donna retreated to his desk off, Linda pulled Lomond aside.

Taking the hint, Torrance and Willie backed away and talked among themselves.

Linda asked Lomond quietly, 'Why did you not want Ross to go out for Murdock?'

Lomond felt no shame in admitting the reason. 'He's got Lachlann at home. I'm not taking any chances. We don't know anything about Walter Murdock. He could be a psychopath for all we know.'

Linda pointed out, 'Pardeep's got three girls at home. Does that not matter to you?'

'Pardeep wasn't just in the hospital from a knife wound because I sent him in somewhere dangerous.'

'That's a rocky road, John. What's next? Keep Ross on desk duty in case he gets in a car accident.'

'That's not the same thing, and you *damn* well know it.' He'd kept his voice down, but not nearly enough to stop Willie and Torrance at least hearing a tone of aggression from him.

'Hey,' Linda warned him. 'Careful. Save that shit for when it's just us.'

He nodded in apology. 'I just...I feel responsible.'

'I know, and you are. But you're also responsible for running your team in such a way that finds and stops bad guys. That doesn't happen if you start pulling your punches, and benching your strongest detectives.'

He relented. 'Okay. Point taken.'

Linda looked around, lowering her voice further. 'So you really think there's something to all this Angela Devlin stuff? You know Torrance has a rep for tin foil hat stuff.'

'It might be a conspiracy theory, but I won't know until I've checked the evidence.' He craned his neck, as Willie held up his phone.

Willie called over, 'Moira's got something.'

Lomond waved to him. 'We'd better go.'

Linda stepped aside, encouraging him to leave. 'Yep. Go.'

Lomond, Willie, and Torrance gathered their things.

Linda turned around to go back up the stairs, relieved that no one could see her gulping hard. And looking nervous. She then took out her phone and tapped out a message.

"I need to see you." She waited for a reply.

"Can't. In a meeting."

"End it."

"What's the problem?"

"Angela Devlin."

There was a pause, then a reply came through.

"Get over here."

Without bothering to take her jacket, Linda hurried out.

Donna was the only one who seemed to notice. 'What's that all about?'

Ross was too busy arranging the dozen open tabs on his computer, while also connecting and reconnecting his phone to the hard drive, in between taking multiple pictures of Jimmy Gribbin's photograph.

Distracted by all of his footering around, Donna asked, 'What are you *doing,* man?'

Ross flicked wildly from tab to tab on the computer. 'Reverse image search.'

'A whatty?' said Donna, using her mum's oft-heard phrase, the term she used whenever she didn't know what something was.

Ross explained it like he was being forced to explain to a two-year-old why two plus two equals four. 'If you capture an image and upload it online, you can run a search to see if that image has appeared anywhere else online before.' He picked up the photo briefly. 'We don't have a lot to work with here...but I think...' He clicked and scrolled and zoomed around the computer screen. 'I think that's it,' he said.

Donna came around behind him for a better look.

He held up the photo that Lomond had taken from the Gribbin's garden shed. He pointed to the edge of a building just about visible in the corner of the photograph. 'Does that...'

he lowered the photo to point to his computer screen. '...look like that to you?'

Donna went back and forth between them.

It was the same crooked oak tree in both images.

She let out a gentle snort as she realised what Ross had found. 'Wait...but what does that mean?'

'It means this dead-end assignment John gave us is no longer a dead-end.'

On Ross's computer screen was an image of a boxy two-storey housing block, incongruous in its design when set against the countryside backdrop. Comparing the building in Jimmy's photo with the image on the screen, it was undeniable that they were the same place.

The caption underneath the online image that Ross had found identified the building as part of Boland Castle hospital.

CHAPTER TWENTY-ONE

JASON CHECKED the address one last time as Pardeep pulled up on Lancaster Crescent.

'This the place?' Pardeep asked.

'Yeah. This one with the black door,' Jason replied.

The street was set back only fifty or so yards from Great Western Road, near its busiest channel between Gartnavel Hospital and Byres Road. Hidden behind a deep and thick wall of bushes and trees, Lancaster Crescent seemed a world away from the hustle and bustle of the busy bus lanes and constant heavy traffic of Great Western Road. It was an oasis of calm.

Elegant blonde sandstone terraced townhouses lined the street, each with expensive cars parked outside, giving the neighbourhood an air of affluence. Despite its proximity to one of the city's main arteries, the leafy seclusion offered a stark contrast to the noise and activity just beyond the greenery.

But as Pardeep and Jason were about to discover, dark things often hide in quiet places.

As the two detective constables approached the house, the quiet of Lancaster Crescent was almost eerie. The tranquillity felt deceptive, a stark counterpoint to the disturbing evidence they were about to uncover.

As he undid his seatbelt, Pardeep remarked, 'How the other half live, eh...'

The men knocked brusquely on the main door of Walter Murdock's address. After a few failed attempts, Jason broke off to peer into the house for signs of activity.

'Anything?' asked Pardeep.

Jason shielded his eyes to see beyond the reflection of the windows. 'Nothing obvious. It looks tidy enough. No coffee cups or plates sitting out. No TV on. No lights.'

Pardeep retreated down the steps, looking left and then right along the street. 'Maybe we could access a garden around the back somehow.'

Then Jason noticed someone standing at the living room window of the house next door. The person gestured that they were coming out.

'I think we've got something,' Jason told Pardeep.

The neighbour came out wearing their slippers, holding a cup of tea. The man was in his late fifties, wearing a flannel shirt that was tucked into his cord trousers. He was well spoken. 'Are you looking for Walter, by any chance?'

Pardeep and Jason showed him their badges.

'I'm Detective Constable Varma, this is Detective Constable Yang,' said Pardeep. 'Do you know if Mr Murdock is home?'

'I'm afraid I don't,' the man replied. 'He hasn't been home for a while.'

'Oh yeah? How long is a while?'

'He left with a large suitcase about a fortnight ago. He told me he was going to Thailand on holiday.'

Pardeep and Jason exchanged a quick glance. But their disappointment was to be short lived.

The man explained, 'I'm his landlord. May I ask what this is regarding?'

'I'm afraid I can't divulge that information, sir,' said Pardeep. 'But I need access to the property. Do you have a key?' Pardeep expected pushback on their lack of a warrant, but was pleasantly surprised when the man quickly turned back inside and returned with a key.

'Do you mind?' The man motioned towards the door, as if he wanted to be the one to open it.

'Go ahead,' Pardeep replied.

Jason asked, 'What's your name, sir?'

'Gerry,' the man answered. 'Gerry McVitie.'

'Are you a full-time landlord, Mr McVitie?' Pardeep asked, masking the leading question.

'Yes,' Gerry answered. 'I'm retired. We – my wife and I – used to own both these addresses. It was a single unit many years ago. We split it up and turned Walter's side into a rental. Lord knows there's enough space for us next door. The kids have long since sailed off to university.' He turned around, proud to emphasise, 'Edinburgh and St Andrew's, the pair of them.'

Once Gerry turned back to the door again, Pardeep rolled his eyes at Jason, as if he was supposed to be impressed at the boast.

'He's not in any trouble, is he? Walter?' Gerry opened the door and held it open for Pardeep and Jason.

'Not yet,' Jason replied, letting Pardeep go first.

Gerry went into landlord mode, as if he was trying to sell the place to prospective tenants. Pointing to each facet as he explained what he'd done to modernise the place.

It might have looked traditional on the outside, but inside it was all chrome and glass furniture.

As they started looking around, through the hallway going into the living room, Pardeep asked, 'Does Mr Murdock live on his own here?'

Gerry, crouching down to inspect a tiny scuff mark on the wooden parquet flooring in the hall, said, 'As far as I'm aware. I don't think I can recall ever seeing him with anyone else.'

Jason remained by Gerry's side, while Pardeep looked around. 'No visitors?' Jason asked.

Gerry stood up, still frowning at the scuff mark. 'No, actually. Never.'

'When did he move into the property?'

'It must be three years ago now. He's probably the best tenant I've ever had. And I've had a lot of properties, believe me. I had twenty-two at one time, in fact. So you can imagine how–'

Impatient with any further boasting, Pardeep interrupted, 'He always pays rent on time? No complaints about him?'

'From me?'

'As you live through the wall. Any strange noises?'

'No, never.' Gerry pointed out around the living room. 'He doesn't even own a TV, or a hi-fi. I never hear anything from him.'

'That must be nice,' Pardeep said distantly, noticing a cupboard door in the corner of the room.

Gerry's stance turned rigid. Defensive now. 'I think I'd like to know what all this is about. I think I'm entitled.'

'No, sir,' Pardeep informed him, as he opened the cupboard door. 'I'm afraid you're not.' Expecting a shallow cupboard inside, Pardeep was taken aback by what he'd found. 'Jason.' He nodded in the direction of the open door.

'What is it?' Jason asked.

'Oh yes,' Gerry said, taking a few quick steps to hurry over. 'I'm quite proud of this one. We knocked through dead space from the hall to put this in...' He paused, as he peeked around behind the door. 'Hmm...I assumed it would be used for storage or something.'

It wasn't just a cupboard. It was an entire room with enough space to take a few steps around in.

Pardeep turned back towards the door, reaching for a light switch.

Above a metal work desk, two overhanging lights switched on. But the light wasn't white or yellow. It was red, and illuminated a surprising sight. What looked like a small laboratory.

'Huh...' said Gerry. 'So that's what he does with all his time. Photography.'

Walter had turned the windowless room into a dark room.

All the essential equipment was present. All of it high end, expensive. From the enlarger – used to protect the negative onto photographic paper – and developer, and contact printer. It was all top of the line, and the room had been maintained immaculately.

Murdock's most recent efforts were still hanging on a wire stretched from one side of the room to the other.

Pardeep and Jason held each other's gaze, trying to not let on how stunned they were.

Pardeep said, 'Seems like he hasn't diversified his subject matter much.'

The photos were all night shots, showing women standing on street corners. All of them similarly lit, bathed in a dark orange haze of Glasgow streetlights. Specifically around the grittier, grimier, and industrial areas of the city. Tradeston. Trongate. Anderston. Duke Street. The quiet streets around the Tennent's brewery. And around Glasgow Green.

The women were all dressed similarly. Short dresses or skirts. Tall boots. Obviously prostitutes.

Gerry didn't know what to think. Or to say. He stammered, 'I don't understand...'

Jason honed in on a series of photos showing the same woman. All appeared to have been taken surreptitiously from inside a car. The woman never showed any signs that she realised she was being photographed. She was just standing around, looking at her phone, smoking cigarettes, or leaning in through car windows to talk to the men inside.

Pardeep took out his phone, using it to point towards the hall. 'Mr McVitie, can I ask you to step back out of this room, please? Thank you...' When he got out into the hall, he called Lomond. 'Walter Murdock is a go on an arrest warrant.'

'You sure?' Lomond checked.

'A hundred per cent,' Pardeep replied. 'And we need to do a welfare check on an as-yet-unidentified female.'

'What are you talking about?'

'He's got a dark room over here. He's been taking pictures of sex workers on the streets without them knowing. They're surveillance shots.' He paused, lowering his voice. 'I think he's been hunting.'

CHAPTER TWENTY-TWO

Torrance was leaning forward in the back seat of Lomond's car like an excited child being taken to a theme park. He was hanging on to the back of Lomond's seat, craning his neck and bobbing and weaving around for just a glimpse of the Scottish Crime Campus from their position on the M73 North at Gartcosh.

'Wait till you see this place,' Willie enthused.

Torrance had retired just a few years before the Campus opening in 2014, but he had seen pictures of it on the news and online. For someone who thought of themselves first and foremost as a detective, Torrance felt like he was making a pilgrimage.

While Lomond and Willie walked swiftly through the car park, Torrance admired the industrial, futuristic design. Raindrops streaking the glass facades from a brief downpour they had just missed. The sunlight reflecting off the wet surfaces gave the building a sleek appearance.

Inside, the architecture was even more extreme, with stairwells and pillars jutting out at funky angles. The last thought on the mind of whoever had picked the furniture was practicality.

While Torrance laboured behind, Lomond muttered to himself as he tried to remember the way. 'I always get lost at this bit,' he said. 'It's like walking through the set of *Blade Runner*.'

Willie smiled politely, missing the movie reference. The only movies Willie had watched – or remembered from his younger days – involved either the Second World War or cockney drug runners.

When they reached the third floor for Forensic Services, the soft sound of music emanated from the direction of Moira McTaggart's laboratory and office.

'What is that?' Willie wondered aloud. 'Is that Fleetwood Mac?'

Lomond smiled with surprise. 'It's "Caravan" by Van Morrison.'

Torrance whispered to Lomond, 'Does Moira always listen to cheery music around dead bodies?'

'I think it lightens the load,' he replied.

When they turned the corner to her office lab, Moira was singing quietly to herself, swaying her hips ever so subtly in time to the music.

At the "la la la-la" part of the chorus, Moira swayed a little more vigorously. Then she realised she had company. Embarrassed, her face flushed a deep red, and she scrambled to turn the music down.

Across the room, Lianne Gribbin's body lay covered over by a white plastic sheet on a metal desk – the dissection table, which came equipped with a drainage system built into the tabletop. A grimly necessary feature for when bodies were pulled out of water sources, often still covered in mud and wet foliage. Scene of crime officers didn't perform clean-up duties before delivering bodies to Moira. Luckily for her she had interns and students to perform such tasks when required.

Moira put a hand to her chest. 'You scared the crap out of me.'

'Sorry,' said Lomond. 'The door was open. Willie said you had something for us.'

As Moira reached for a pair of latex gloves from a large box – like an enormous box of jumbo tissues – Lomond gave Willie a wee nudge, then nodded at Moira. Lomond then gestured and mouthed, 'Ring.'

Willie leaned forward in surprise as he clocked the engagement ring on Moira's finger, then the pair smiled at each other.

With her back to the men, Moira walked over to Lianne's body. 'What are you girls giggling about amongst yourselves?'

'Nothing,' Willie said.

She retorted, 'It's a sad day when something as trite as a ring on a woman's finger reduces two of Police Scotland's best to gossiping teenagers.' She turned to Torrance. 'I see at least Bob here has the decency to behave like a grown-up instead of crowing about an engagement.'

Torrance lit up in delight. 'You're engaged? That's fantastic, Moira. Congrats.'

She rolled her eyes as she took up a position next to the body. 'Moving on, shall we...' She pulled the sheet back off the body without any airs or graces. As far as she was concerned, anyone who couldn't handle the realities of dead bodies had no business being in the room.

The only positive was not having to cope with the usual smell that came with dead bodies.

As the men stepped closer, they noticed a faint, musty odour. Only Lomond had experience of it in the past. A unique blend of earthiness and only a subtle scent of decay. The harsh, sharp mineral-like notes that normally accompanied body decomposition were all but gone. In their place was a smell of aged, dry bone that brought to mind an old, dusty attic, along with a faint smell of damp earth or clay – lingering remnants of the body's interment.

Lomond, curious about the smell, said, 'I thought the body bag she was in was airtight.'

'Yes, but twenty years, John. The plastic wasn't entirely impregnable. The subtle shifting and movement of earth around the bag created microscopic holes. Over that length of time, enough molecules are able to penetrate and colour the smell of the bones.

The smell left Lomond depressed. It was the smell of an ancient, forgotten presence, rather than the more immediate and pungent odours that came with fresh bodies. It only served to reinforce to Lomond the fact that Lianne had been lost to time, and that he would do everything in his power to bring her killer to justice.

'What are we looking at, then?' he asked.

Moira asked, 'What do you want first?'

'Cause of death?'

'I'm about as certain as I can be that it was by strangulation.' She passed Lomond a plastic evidence bag containing the horse bridle. 'After examination under the microscope, you can see where the material has been unnaturally stretched and stressed.'

Willie asked, 'And that wouldn't come from ordinary use?'

'Not to this degree. The material has puckered in such a way that only huge physical force could have caused it.' She pointed to the neck bones using a thin metal bone saw, then offered her loupe to Lomond.

She had already detached it from her glasses, allowing Lomond to use it like a regular magnifying glass.

'The hyoid bone fractures and damage to the vertebrae in the neck,' Moira said. 'Those are consistent with strangulation.'

Lomond stood up and offered the loupe to Willie, who took it.

'That seems quite pronounced,' he said.

'It is,' she replied. 'Whoever killed her is strong. The force necessary to inflict that sort of damage to the bones...the killer must have been in a state of extreme anger.'

Torrance suggested, 'Or extreme determination.' Sensing that the others wanted him to elaborate, he added, 'Saying it was borne out of anger suggests someone out of control. Blinded by rage. I don't think that's who our guy is.'

Moira said, 'Well, there's no skin to examine, of course. But I'm comfortable declaring this a murder victim.'

Lomond asked, 'What about confirmation of identity?'

'We have DNA samples taken from Lianne Gribbin's clothing found at her residence at the time of her disappearance. Detectability over such a long period of time decreases significantly. But thanks to the diligent wrapping around the body, I've been able to recover enough DNA to conclude positively that this is the body of Lianne Gribbin.'

In a way, Lomond felt relieved that Lianne's mum would at least have confirmation, and that Brenda wouldn't die without ever knowing what happened to her daughter. But the manner of the death wasn't going to be easy to describe to her.

Moira went on, 'I haven't got into any further dating on the body yet. That's going to take a little more time.'

'It doesn't really matter,' said Lomond. 'Either way, we know what we're dealing with now. Lianne Gribbin was murdered.'

Torrance piped up behind. 'John,' he said softly. 'Um... what about...'

Remembering their discussion from the car, Lomond took out his phone and found the investigation code. 'Yeah, Moira. We've got another one we need to get some information on. Tricia Dunn.'

Moira retreated to her computer, removing her gloves on the way. She opened up her computer application for access to her forensics version of Crimson. An enhanced version of the HOLMES system – a database used by UK police forces for managing and sharing information in large-scale investigations – Crimson offered advanced features particular to Moira's job. At her fingertips, with the relevant enquiry code, she could access forensics data from years earlier.

Moira clicked her tongue rapidly while she skimmed the enquiry notes. 'This one was before my time,' she said. Noticing the use of a horse bridle on the victim, same as Lianne Gribbin, Moira remarked, 'Hmm, tasty.'

She might have been lighter in tone, and more prone to singing in her office these days, but at heart she was still the Moira that officers still referred to as Moira Dreich.

'Plenty of overlap,' she said, backing away from the computer screen. 'Are you thinking serial?'

'Yeah,' Lomond confirmed.

'It's certainly possible based on what's here.'

Willie asked, 'But why the burying?'

'Yeah,' said Torrance. 'Tricia Dunn was practically left in the street. Her body was barely cold when she was found.'

Staring at Lianne's skeleton, Lomond replied, 'I think Lianne was his first. He didn't know yet if one would be enough. And he didn't want to get caught before he found out. Then he wanted more.'

'But why all the weird horse stuff?' Willie asked.

The room turned silent for a few moments, then Moira suggested, 'What about kelpies?'

'The big horse statues?' said Willie.

'No, as in the actual folklore.' Moira pushed herself back off her stool to consult her considerable library of books. After a brief search, she pulled out a volume of Scottish folklore. She turned to a chapter which documented the shape-shifting, horse-like creatures. She pointed to portraits of woman draped over rocks next to rivers and lochs. 'Kelpies,' she explained, 'also have the ability, it's said, to transform themselves into non-equine forms such as alluring women. The kelpies would retain this form until a man was tempted close to them. They would then shape-shift back into their equine form. Some kelpies are said to be equipped with tack, such as a bridle, a bit, and sometimes a saddle. So went the folklore to beware of alluring women found near bodies of water, for fear they would turn into kelpies and drown you. It was said that if you ever encountered such a creature, the only way to kill it was by…' Moira looked up to deliver the conclusion. 'Suffocating it. Either by drowning, or strangulation.'

Lomond said, 'You think there's some kind of game being played out?'

'Perhaps of a man drifting into temptation. A temptation he's tried all his life to refuse. Maybe this act is his only way of reasserting control.'

Willie said, 'But the water thing doesn't really add up, does it?'

Lomond replied, 'Lianne was found right next to the Clyde. She was known to have worked around Anderston near the riverside.'

'What about Tricia Dunn? She was found near Trongate.'

Torrance shut his eyes, as if they had the answer they were looking for. 'She was picked up a few times for solicitation near the Saltmarket.'

Lomond said, 'The riverside again.'

'Maybe the killer picked her up near the riverside before taking her to the Trongate area where it was quieter.'

Lomond took out his phone, seeing that Pardeep was calling.

When he answered, Torrance and Willie watched with anticipation, hoping for good news.

The phone signal was a little weak where they were, causing Lomond to strain to make out what Pardeep was saying.

Lomond asked, 'Photos of who?'

Returning to her paperwork, Moira said to Torrance and Willie, 'Let me guess. You're all about to run out of here with a sense of urgency.'

Willie answered stoically, 'Yeah, probably.'

Lomond lowered the phone. 'Guys, we're going.'

Once the men hustled out of the office, Moira put Van Morrison back on, resuming where "Caravan" had paused earlier. 'You're welcome,' she said to no one.

CHAPTER TWENTY-THREE

Chief Superintendent Alasdair Reekie was pacing the length of his expansive office which overlooked Richmond Park on the other side of the River Clyde. The corner office was one of the most sought-after in Police Scotland's administrative headquarters in Dalmarnock. But Reekie couldn't think of anywhere else he'd less like to be.

He had already spotted Linda pulling in to the car park – her aged Honda Civic taking its rightful place in the hierarchy, parking alongside the secretaries and other mid-tier administrative staff. In Helen Street, Linda Boyle was a big deal. In the place they called Mordor, she was a small fish in a very big pond.

She stormed past Reekie's secretary, who stood up to stop her.

'It's fine, Alison,' Reekie explained. 'Linda doesn't need to be on the list.' He tried to force a smile at her as she came in. 'Do you, Linda?' His smile vanished the moment the door closed behind him.

Linda paced back and forth, like a caged dog waiting to be let out. 'I told you this would come back to bite us,' she said.

'You mentioned Angela Devlin in your message,' Reekie said. 'Why don't you walk me through it. From the start.'

Linda prowled in front of his desk. 'John's been doing some digging on what happened to Angela Devlin.'

'How? Why?'

'Because of Bob Torrance.'

Reekie scoffed. 'Bob Torrance? That's a blast from the past. What's he doing around?'

'He's been working with Serious Crime Review on a cold case, and he's convinced it's connected to Angela Devlin.'

Reekie returned to his chair and leaned back.

'You look pretty relaxed right now, considering what's on the line here.'

'No, I'm pretty far from relaxed,' he said, 'but it won't do us any good to get into a flap.' He passed, tapping on his armrest. 'Okay, what does John actually know?'

'Everything.'

'He can't know everything. If he knew everything, we wouldn't be having this conversation.'

'He knows that there was a cover-up in the Devlin case. That there were judges, senior officials in the CPS, and Police Scotland involved.'

'But no names yet?'

Linda looked at him like he was crazy. 'Well, no, not yet. But John's only had it a matter of hours. It's John! He's going to break it wide open eventually.'

'I wish you'd told me that before you came all the way over here. I was under the impression that he actually knew something. There's a world of difference between eventually and now. I've spent most of the day mopping up after John's political calamity this morning, shutting down construction on the bridge.'

'How long do you think it's going to take – with Bob's help – to uncover that it was you who buried Bob's report about the Devlin case?'

Reekie pouted and gave a stern shake of his head. 'My conscience is clear on that one. It wasn't that I actually knew certain individuals had abused children, and I helped them not get caught. I might be ambitious, but I'm not a monster, Linda. There was no proof in what Torrance was saying. He said that judges and these senior police officials were involved in a cover-up, but there wasn't any evidence to say that definitively that was the case. It was all circumstantial, hearsay, and, frankly, a lot of bollocks doled out by Bruce bloody Murdock. None of it could be published without any evidence. I told Bob that, and he refused to accept it. So I buried his report. The old prick should have thanked me. I got him another ten years on his career because of that. If we had published that report of his, it would have ended him.'

Linda fired back, 'But it was in your interests to kill the report, though. Wasn't it? Same as it's in your interest to keep it hidden now.'

'I don't know what you mean,' he replied with a nervous sniff.

'Everyone knows you're being touted to take over from Brendan as Assistant Chief Constable for the West. And Brendan's shooting for the top spot at Tulliallan. The last thing anyone needs is a lot of headlines about any of the executive team being linked to a cover-up of child abusers and rampant use of sex workers.' She paused to see if Reekie had anything to say.

But he just sat there.

Linda continued, 'This is what's wrong with the world now. Everyone's incentivised to do bad things. To lie. To say whatever you have to if it ensures a pay day. That's what's wrong with the system, Alasdair. You knew that doing a favour for powerful people would be in your interest someday. This is how it all goes wrong. It's not people sitting in offices, conspiring to off people. It's conversations like this, conspiring against good people, decent people like John and Bob Torrance. It's not about justice. It's just a series of transactions among the rich and powerful, with those who operate under the delusion that one day they'll be rich and powerful too. And all they have to do is wait to be invited up to their table. But here's the thing, Alasdair. That invitation isn't coming. People like you and me, we do all their dirty work. We shovel their shit. And for what? So they can pull the ladder up behind them as they go?'

'I've got a family just like you,' said Reekie. 'I know I don't have your respect, but I'd hope I could at least get your understanding.'

'Sometimes saying nothing can have just as bad an effect as a knife or a gun.'

'We don't know who did any of this. Who killed Tricia Dunn, or Lianne Gribbin. Or who was behind the conspiracy that robbed Angela Devlin of justice.'

'See, I think we do,' Linda replied. 'We just haven't found the evidence yet. We knew it back then and we still know it.'

Reekie paused. His mask of emotional impenetrability slipping. 'If you want to prove something extraordinary, it requires extraordinary evidence.'

'How?'

Reekie considered the options. 'Tell John to do whatever is necessary. Just make sure he gets the proof. If this is weak in any way, it'll bury the lot of us.'

CHAPTER TWENTY-FOUR

Back at Lancaster Crescent, police presence was considerably more noticeable than earlier. Gerry McVitie stood helplessly on his front steps as more uniform officers poured into the property as darkness descended.

Pardeep, now furnished with a warrant, directed them to various rooms in search of anything suspicious that might possibly relate to a murder.

Jason was in the hall, finishing up a phone call with HM Passport Office's dedicated unit for liaising with police enquiries. 'Okay, thanks,' he said, hanging up.

'Anything?' asked Pardeep, but he knew from the downbeat tone of Jason's voice.

'There's been no action on Walter Murdock's passport,' said Jason. 'If he's gone to Thailand like the neighbour says, then it's not been on his own passport.

'Shite,' Pardeep cursed to himself. 'The gaffer's going to be here any minute. I was hoping to have at least something for him.' He looked all around, watching the constables combing through Murdock's living room, bedroom, kitchen, dining room, office. Emptying drawers, turning out cupboards, removing every item from sideboards and units and bookcases.

Nothing of note anywhere.

Pardeep then turned sharply, looking straight down the hall towards a bathroom. He sniffed. 'Do you smell that?'

'What?' Jason asked.

Pardeep marched down the hall towards the bathroom and opened the door fully. He sniffed again. Harder this time. 'Can you not smell that?'

Jason sniffed now. It took him a few seconds to realise the implications. 'Oh crap.'

'Yeah, oh crap,' said Pardeep. He turned the main light on, which filled the room crystalline white.

At a glance, the room appeared to be immaculate – much as the rest of the property. But a much closer inspection revealed straight faint streaks in the bath's enamel.

'What is that?' asked Jason, wondering what Pardeep was scratching at.

'It's the same as on the sink.' He crouched down to look under the sink, shining the light from his phone onto the underside. 'Call Moira McTaggart,' he said.

'Are you sure?'

Pardeep got quickly to his feet. 'I'm sure.'

Just then, Lomond, Willie, and Torrance arrived at the front entrance.

'What have we got, boys?' asked Lomond.

Jason deferred to his more experienced colleague.

Pardeep hurried back down the hall to greet them. He said, 'Murdock's gone. Done a runner. The neighbour reckons he went to Thailand, but Jason's had confirmation there's been no action on Murdock's passport.'

Willie asked, 'Is the neighbour lying?'

'I don't think so. And get this. At first, the neighbour said Murdock left the house with a suitcase and said where he was going. But that wasn't quite right.' Pardeep gestured for Jason to take over.

Jason said, 'The neighbour now says that Murdock was carrying a flight case with wheels. And it looked very heavy.'

'Daytime or night-time?' Lomond asked, leaning forward in anticipation.

Jason couldn't help but grin. 'Night-time. The neighbour thinks about eleven. Says Murdock seemed rattled and nervous. And that the case was so heavy, he could barely lift it. When he offered to help Murdock carry it, Murdock got angry and told him he didn't need any help. Despite the fact he was apparently, quote, late for his flight to Thailand.'

Willie looked expectantly at Lomond. 'We need to find this guy and bring him in.'

'I'll say,' Lomond replied.

'That's not all,' said Pardeep, turning in profile to leave a clear view down the hall towards the bathroom.

As Lomond was about to enter, Pardeep handed him a pair of latex gloves. The moment he walked in, the smell knocked Lomond back.

'Jesus...' Lomond said, not wanting to breathe through his nose. 'So bleach must have been on multibuy, then.'

Willie put his hand to his nose. 'Christ, someone's been busy in here.'

Pardeep explained, 'I noticed the smell, then found white stains on the bath. He's been using something that's far too strong for enamel. If you look closely, you can see what I think are the bristles of a brush where he's been scrubbing.'

Lomond leaned down to inspect it. 'Yep...looks like it.'

Pardeep then pointed Lomond towards what he'd found under the sink.

There were pinkish splatter marks, and some faded lines.

'Does that look like blood to you?' Pardeep asked.

Lomond looked closely. 'Yes, it does,' he replied. He pointed to the various stains one at a time. 'You've got your run off, from overflowing out of the sink and running down the edge. Then you've got these.' He moved aside to let Willie in. 'Do those look like splatter marks to you?'

Willie crouched down with a deep groan. 'Looks like it.'

Torrance suggested, 'We should get Moira over here.'

'She's on her way,' said Pardeep.

'Good job, son,' Lomond said, patting him on the shoulder.

Pardeep showed no emotion, but inside he was dancing. A pat on the shoulder was Lomond's equivalent of taking him out to a football match for a pie and a pint.

Lomond stood up fully, taking in the possibilities. 'Maybe there was a struggle. Someone on the floor for there to be splatters on the underside of the sink.'

'Maybe Moira will get us a match,' Torrance suggested.

'Maybe,' Lomond said, unconvinced. 'I've got a feeling we might find a body before we get a match on that blood.' As he peeled his gloves off in the hall, Lomond looked around, taking in all the unfamiliar faces that were milling around in the property. He looked like he had lost something. 'Where's Ross and Donna?' he asked.

CHAPTER TWENTY-FIVE

Ross and Donna were now side by side at his desk in similar states of undress. Ross's sleeves were now rolled up, tie loosened. Donna's suit jacket was off, and her top shirt button undone. Both of them were leaning towards the screen, compelled to press on with each new discovery.

They had a host of resources at their fingerprints. More than enough to find out every job Jimmy Gribbin had ever had. Where he had lived. Where he had travelled to. What he'd spent money on.

In a few hours, Donna and Ross had found his entire employment history through Jimmy's National Insurance records. HMRC's dedicated police assistance portal gave them access to his tax payments, list of employers through the years, as well as a general financial history. They had the Electoral Register. Council Tax records. Public records of property ownership. Credit Reference Agencies, as well as the Department of Work and Pensions, which detailed benefits claimed in a lifetime.

And it made for interesting reading.

'Look at this,' said Ross, eyes wide with wonder. 'From nineteen seventy-eight, all the way through to the late nineties, his employer is listed as Westbury Burnham.'

'Who are they?' asked Donna.

'They were a contractor for the NHS across central Scotland.'

'I thought Jimmy was a joiner by trade.'

'He was,' said Ross. He clicked over to the DWP tab and scrolled down. 'Look at what Jimmy put down for workplace address from the early nineties through to his retirement.'

'Boland Castle hospital.'

'He was the on-site handyman.'

After doing some quick maths, Donna said, 'He was there at the time Angela Devlin went there.'

'And Tricia Dunn.'

'But hang on, hang on...' Donna shook her head rapidly. 'Angela Devlin was groomed by a gang in Edinburgh. We haven't found anything linking Jimmy to Edinburgh.'

'True,' Ross admitted.

'And the one link we had between Angela Devlin's abuse case and the murders of Tricia and Lianne, is that Angela and Tricia both went to Boland Castle. And both Tricia and Lianne stayed in Copeland House hostel as adults.'

Ross clicked over to another tab. 'That's what we thought. But I've just found this.'

Donna leaned forward. 'No,' she exclaimed.

'Lianne Gribbin was a resident in Boland Castle between the age of fourteen and sixteen.'

Donna leaned back in her chair, stunned. 'But that changes everything.'

'I don't know that it changes everything. It certainly changes the notion that the only man linking Tricia Dunn and Lianne Gribbin is Walter Murdock.'

CHAPTER TWENTY-SIX

Walter Murdock's residence on Lancaster Crescent was now a full-blown crime scene. A white tent had been erected over the front entrance, to protect the integrity of the house, controlling movement of officers in and out, and ensuring protective foot coverings, gloves, and masks were worn in and around the bathroom area.

It was still unknown exactly what had happened in there, but Moira McTaggart was on the scene to investigate.

Lomond appeared in the hallway holding a takeaway coffee that a young constable had fetched for him on Hyndland Road. He slipped his mask up to allow access to the cup.

Even with her back turned, Moira warned him, 'Don't think I can't see what you're doing back there.'

Lomond looked around, mystified, and mouthed to himself, 'How?'

She backed away from the sink, where she'd been taking samples from the blood splatters. She lowered the hood on her paper suit. She said, 'You'd be as well ditching that coffee for some tea with honey, because there's no way I'm going to have anything useful for you until the morning.'

'That's okay,' Lomond answered. 'I don't sleep much anyway. Do you have any idea what went down in there?'

Moira bobbed her head from side to side. 'Judging by the pattern of the blood splatter, I'd say that someone was opened up pretty well in here.'

'Really?'

Moira asked him to step back, then turned off the light. She then turned on her dark light, which showed the extent of what they were dealing with.

'Dear god,' Lomond winced.

The floor was almost entirely covered by a single dark stain illuminated by the dark light.

'It doesn't matter what they use,' Moira said. 'It always shows up.'

Recoiling from the sight, Lomond said, 'That's a hell of a lot of blood someone lost.'

'Which is what makes me suspect there was a murder here. Fairly recently, I'd say. The smell of the chemicals he's used to clean up would fade within about four to five days, even with the window shut. Has anyone told you about the bucket outside?'

'No,' replied Lomond.

'One of my techs found a metal bucket out in the back garden. It contains remnants of burned clothes.'

'He did his best to be thorough.'

'It all leaves a trace.' Moira switched the dark light off, and put on the overhead lights again. 'Get some rest, John. It's been a long day.'

He took a sip of coffee. 'I can't. I've got a briefing next door.'

The Major Investigations Team had assembled in Walter

Murdock's living room, and were all talking enthusiastically over one another, sharing opinions and leads.

Ross and Donna's progress update was the one Lomond wanted to hear first. When they were done, the group collectively held their breath.

Lomond looked around his team. 'What do we think?'

'It doesn't fit,' said Ross.

'Why not?'

'Jimmy doesn't fit the profile of this kind of murderer. In any case, we're sitting here talking about this mere yards away from a dark room containing photos that prove how obsessed with prostitutes Murdock was. Those aren't loving portraits. They're surveillance shots. He's hunting.'

'Speaking of which,' said Lomond, 'how close are we to identifying the woman?'

Jason answered, 'I'm liaising with a team working on it back at Helen Street.'

Lomond pointed out one of the photos lying on the coffee table in front of them. 'It's not good enough, Jason. This woman is next, if it isn't her blood all over the bathroom already. For all we know, it's the reason that Murdock's missing. Lord knows he's not a flight to Thailand. No chance.'

Torrance said, 'Have I mentioned that I don't think Murdock is our killer?'

'Well, you have now,' Willie remarked. 'What makes you so sure, in light of the evidence?'

'None of the victims so far show any signs of being cut. What happened in the bathroom was big and messy. That's not our guy's style.'

'True,' Lomond admitted. 'Until we can track down Murdock's location, I want us to pivot to Jimmy Gribbin.'

Addressing Ross, he said, 'I want a full timeline of Jimmy's whereabouts versus the women who disappeared.'

'From twenty years ago?' asked Ross.

'If we're going to go down this road, I want to make sure that nothing boneheaded shows up. Like Jimmy being out of the country for weeks either side of a disappearance.' He looked at Donna. 'What about Lianne?'

Donna said, 'Her medical records show that she was a patient at Boland Castle for a spell. Somewhere between fourteen and sixteen.'

'I told you something happened to her. A sudden change in her mid-teens.'

Torrance suggested, 'Maybe it's time to talk to Brenda again.'

Lomond shook his head. 'She was only told this morning that her daughter was killed. Let's give her the courtesy of twenty-four hours to herself before we wade in again. In any case, if Jimmy was the killer, he died years ago.'

'But what if it's not Jimmy?' said Torrance. 'Then the clock is probably ticking for someone else, and we'd have no idea about it.'

Lomond relented. 'It's possible.'

CHAPTER TWENTY-SEVEN

It was dark enough outside now for Barry to feel comfortable taking the flight case to the car. The car that his brother didn't know about. It was a white saloon in terrible condition. But somehow it had lasted him more than twenty years.

He liked it. It was cheap to run. He got good mileage.

But most of all because it had a deceptively large boot.

The flight case was on wheels, so transporting it along the pavement was no problem. But lifting it down stairs, and into the car boot was quite another matter.

Inside the case, the woman made a faint screeching sound. The only version of a scream that she could muster now.

Barry took a good look around. The street was deserted, and he was bathed in darkness under the thick canopy of overhanging trees. He rested a hand on top of the case and leaned down closer so that she could hear him.

'Have you still got the bit in your mouth?' he asked. 'I hope so. That's the best part. The metal bar. How it feels against your tongue. Cold. And when you feel that bridle around your face, and you realise you're no longer in control. That's why I do it this way. I'm setting you free. Do you see that? It's my way of telling you how much I love you. To dress you the same way as the horses. They're so beautiful. You should see them running in the dark. Have you ever ridden a horse in the dark?' He paused. 'I bet you haven't. I remember the first time I did it. He showed me how. Jimmy. After the first time, it was so easy. I took control of the reins, and when I pulled, the horse stopped. Have you any idea how it feels...to be in control of something so powerful? They hold this sway over me, you see. This is my way of setting them free. And setting myself free. So that nothing – no one – can take control of me again.' He lifted his hand from the lid of the case. 'I promise I'll make it easy on you. You've been one of the good ones.'

Inside, the woman was sobbing. Convinced that she was living out her final hours.

Barry explained, 'I just want to set you free. It won't be much longer now.'

CHAPTER TWENTY-EIGHT

Lomond felt terrible knocking on Brenda Gribbin's door again, but he didn't think he had a choice.

Brenda was gracious, and assumed that Lomond had come back to relay new information about Lianne. So she was surprised to discover that he had come back to ask more questions.

Lomond had brought Donna again for consistency. And as Brenda had apparently warmed to her presence earlier on.

'What have you found?' Brenda asked, steeling herself for graphic details.

Lomond said, 'I actually had a few questions I wanted to ask about Jimmy.'

'Jimmy? What's he got to do with anything?'

'I couldn't help but notice how different the house looks, compared to what it was years ago. There's a lot of photographs of him missing, and I was wondering if it might be related to some new information that's come to light.'

'What sort of information?' she asked.

Lomond could tell that Brenda was right on the edge. Her

face was much tenser than earlier in the day. She hadn't prepared herself for the visit either. She was wearing her dressing gown and slippers, already prepared for an early night, which made her feel vulnerable in the presence of the two officers.

'Mrs Gribbin,' Lomond began, 'it's time for us to tell you about another enquiry that we've been working on. It's another murder, and it goes back six years. A woman called Tricia Dunn. She was a sex worker in the city centre and riverside areas, mostly. It's our belief that whoever killed her may also be responsible for the death of Lianne.' He paused. 'Our investigation has now progressed to the stage where we're confident in declaring it a murder enquiry.'

Brenda whimpered. Raising her hand to her mouth. 'Oh god...'

'There are several important points connecting the two enquiries. But one of them is a shared connection to Boland Castle hospital.' It wasn't just for effect that Lomond paused. He wanted to gauge her reaction.

She didn't appear surprised. 'I see.'

'Specifically,' Lomond elaborated, 'the fact that Jimmy was employed there for so long.'

All of a sudden, Brenda wilted. She buried her face in her hands and began to cry.

Lomond shared a quick glance with Donna. 'Brenda,' he continued, 'is there anything you can tell me about the circumstances that led to Lianne being hospitalised at Boland Castle?'

Brenda searched up her sleeves for a tissue, but didn't have any.

Donna had a few prepared in her pocket, and handed her one.

'It was Jimmy's idea,' she sobbed gently. 'She had changed

so suddenly, I didn't know what to do. She wouldn't talk to me. She was a different person. Jimmy said that the hospital was a really good place for young people like Lianne to start over. That they used this ECT thing. You know, electro-shock. He said the doctors reckoned they could help her.' She shook her head, and cried harder this time. 'So I agreed. Jimmy took her in. And for the next eighteen months, I watched my wee girl disintegrate to almost nothing. That's when the drugs started. In that place.'

Lomond stayed quiet, letting Donna take over for the next part as agreed.

Donna said, 'Brenda, you mentioned this sudden change that came over Lianne. In our experience that can mean a number of different things. But one of them is that it can be a symptom of child sexual abuse. Did you ever have any concerns that Jimmy might have done something to Lianne?'

Brenda was no longer crying. The tears replaced with a hardened expression. 'I had concerns. You could say that, yes. The problem was, I was drinking a lot then. I wasn't in any fit state to...' She broke off, distraught at the notion that her alcohol dependency could have contributed to her own daughter's abuse. 'The hospital was nothing like how Jimmy described it. He'd made it sound like this country retreat. But when I went there to see Lianne one day, it was like an open prison. There were kids running about the place. No one supervising. A lot of them seemed to be on a lot of medication. They weren't fit to be on their own, half of them. Lianne wasn't much better. Anyway, I told Jimmy that I thought we should get her out. I had finally cut out drinking, and wanted us all to start fresh. But he got so angry. He said that we couldn't take her out now. That it would ruin everything. All of her progress. It was madness. Anyone could see that she was a shell of who she used to be. I thought maybe there was a reason he wanted her to be kept in that state.'

Donna asked, 'Were there other girls like Lianne at the hospital?'

'Dozens,' Brenda replied. 'They were all loaded up on meds for visiting time. So one time I brought a notebook for her. I told her that I thought she was able to understand me just fine. But that the meds made it hard for her to speak her mind. That was what the notebook was for. And if she ever wanted to tell me something, she could write it down in that.'

Lomond, who was nearing the end of a very long day, crept forward in his seat. 'Did she ever write anything in it?'

'She wrote loads,' Brenda replied.

'Do you still have it?'

Brenda nodded. 'I can get it for you if you like.'

Lomond somehow managed to answer with a simple 'please', giving away none of the anticipation he was feeling.

While Brenda was gone, Lomond whispered to Donna, 'This should be interesting.'

When she returned with the notebook, she had already turned to a certain page. 'You might find this passage...I don't know. I thought you should read it.'

Lomond took the notebook. As he started reading, his heart was pounding. He had spent some time with officers who dealt with evidence involving child abuse offences. The officers had told him, it didn't matter how much experience they had. Every piece of evidence had the potential to leave them shaken. For what Lianne was describing, Lomond could barely comprehend it.

The passage talked about strange men coming into Lianne's room soon after her ECT sessions. They were long and painful sessions, and they left her brain foggy. But Lianne could still describe different men's voices. Accents. Their smells. Some spoke with posh accents, according to Lianne's account. She was told that certain men were very important, and that she was to do as they asked.

Brenda, who was already familiar with the material, stared into space while Lomond read.

When he reached the end of the passage, Lomond handed it to Donna. 'Brenda, from what I've read here tonight, I can tell you that a lot of fits with a certain avenue we're exploring.' Lomond left a heavy pause dangling in the air. 'And I have to tell you is that we have not yet ruled out Jimmy as a suspect. In either the death of Lianne. Or Tricia Dunn.'

'Brenda,' Donna said, 'Can we take this notebook of Lianne's away with us for evidence? It will be returned to you as soon as we no longer need it. But as part of the enquiry, we need to make thorough notes about some of the details in this.'

Brenda nodded.

She managed to hold it together, at least until Lomond and Donna had left.

The pair could hear her sobbing from the front garden.

'That was unpleasant,' said Donna, getting into the car.

Lomond sighed once he was in the driver's seat.

'You okay?' asked Donna.

'Yeah,' he replied. 'It just means that Bob Torrance is almost certainly right about his conspiracy theory.'

CHAPTER TWENTY-NINE

Now that his son Lachlann had turned two years old, breakfast time had become the only reliable period where Ross and Isla could be together with him. By the time he got home from nursery and had dinner, it was practically bedtime. And after that – assuming that neither was working – Ross and Isla were both so shattered, they would both invariably spend half an hour picking something to watch on Netflix, only for both of them to fall asleep before the opening credits.

Lachlann had demanded to listen to 'the holiday lady', which Ross knew from experience meant Billie Holiday. Somehow, Lachlann had developed a fondness for her track "For All We Know".

Isla sat down with a bowl of cereal. 'I'm just relieved it's not...' she mouthed the rest. '"The Wheels on the Bus." Why does the mummy on the bus say shush shush shush, while the daddy gets to say I love you? Not very fair. I mean, how did the song come into the public consciousness anyway? It's not like it was a big single.'

Laughing, Ross set down Lachlann's porridge, then his

own. 'That's a lot of thought you've put into that song, Isla. You know what I don't understand? Why the song "Three Blind Mice" is okay. Cutting off tails with a carving knife? I mean, come on. It's perverse.'

'Perverse?' said Isla with a full mouth.

'No song for children should glorify knife crime.'

She burst out laughing, then realises he was serious. 'Are you for real?'

Ross paused. 'Not as much as you're hoping.'

'Ross, you can't shelter him from everything. At a certain point, the world has to find its way in to his personal space. It's part of growing up.'

Without Ross realising it, Lachlann had grabbed the phone and had somehow managed to put on a version of "A Sailor Went to Sea".

'Oh god help us,' Ross complained, recoiling at the nasally voice, and the singer's forced wackiness. 'He's like one of those dads at soft play that only knows how to entertain their kid by being loud and falling over.'

'Lachlann likes it when you fall over,' Isla pointed out.

Ross scrolled to the keypad on his phone, then held it up in front of Lachlann's face. 'Right, matey...can you tell daddy where the number nine is?'

Confused, Isla asked, 'Why the number nine?'

Lachlann pressed the first button he laid eyes on.

'No,' said Ross. 'So number nine is this one. Can you press it three times?'

As the penny dropped, Isla laughed in amazement. 'Are you really trying to teach him how to dial nine nine nine?'

'It's a sensible move, Isla.'

She dusted off the last spoonfuls on the move towards the

kitchen, then kissed Ross on top of the head. 'So is John ever going to call Catriona?'

'Oh jeez, Isla, I don't know. Gonna not put me in the position of pushing my boss into a date he doesn't want to go on?'

'You said he was ready.'

'I said I thought he was ready. It seems I was wrong.'

While she spoke, Isla managed to perform several tasks for Lachlann at what appeared to be the same time. 'He thinks he doesn't deserve happiness – *that's* his problem.'

'Maybe,' Ross muttered.

'Well, if you think he's ready, why don't you give him a gentle nudge to meet up with her? It's not good for him to only have work in his life.'

Lachlann threw down his spoon and announced, 'You did do a po-oo-ooh,' giving the word at least three syllables.

'Okay, buddy,' Ross said, unfazed.

Lachlann's habit of confusing I and you was so frequent that Ross and Isla had stopped noticing it.

As Isla dashed to the hall for her jacket, she called back, 'You've got two jobs today, Ross. Look after yourself. And tell John to call Catriona.' As she opened the front door she was greeted with an enormous rubbish bag that she had left there the night before, but had been too afraid to unlock the door to take it out for fear of it waking Lachlann. 'Damn,' she said, stepping over the rubbish bag. 'Okay, three things for you to do today.'

Once they were alone, Ross faced the mad dash to somehow get himself and Lachlann ready at the same time. Just when he thought it was safe to turn his back for all of ten seconds to swash some mouthwash, Lachlann decided to stand up on the living room sofa, then threw himself down. He let out a joyful cackle when he landed on his bottom. The next time he attempted it, Ross saw the danger immediately.

Lachlann jumped up, but instead of landing flat on the cushion, he had gone up at a slight angle, which meant he was going to hit the backrest on his way down, which would then throw him forward, and launch him head-first off the edge of the couch.

Too far from the sink to spit out the mouthwash so he could shout a warning, Ross had no option but to swallow it. But it tasted so bad he couldn't shout the warning anyway.

Ross threw himself towards the couch, managing to get a cushion onto the floor for Lachlann to land on safely.

But the worst was still to come.

With time running out, Ross grabbed his house key, preparing to take to the rubbish out from the porch. But then he forgot his phone. Then he didn't have enough hands to lift the rubbish bag.

He groaned, trying to lift it with one hand. A fatal error. His fingers ripped right through the plastic, tearing a long hole in the side, where the most rotten, foul, wet rubbish in the bag came pouring out.

He somehow managed to drag the bag close enough to the bins to officially qualify as having "taken the rubbish out", then he turned back to the house. Only to be greeted by the sight of Lachlann standing in the doorway, pushing the front door closed.

'Bye bye, daddy,' he announced.

Ross was still yards away from the door. He reached out in desperation and yelled, 'No no no, hands off...'

But it was already too late. The door had clicked shut.

He shut his eyes, in the grips of a full-on panic. 'Oh please, no. Oh please, no...' he mumbled to himself, patting himself down. He waited for the miraculous heft of feeling his keys in a pocket somewhere. Then remembered he had ditched them in the doorway to get his shoes changed. Of course, he blamed Isla for the disaster. If she hadn't demanded no outdoor shoes in the house, he wouldn't have had to put his keys down, and he wouldn't be locked out now.

And their child wouldn't be locked in a house on his own.

Ross ran to the door, trying – and failing – to sound calm. 'Hey Lachlann! Hey, buddy. Now, you stay here by the door for me, okay? Daddy just needs to phone someone.'

In the circumstances, there was only one person he could trust for help.

CHAPTER THIRTY

LOMOND PULLED up in his car and hurried over to Ross, who was issuing instructions through the living room window for a game for Lachlann to play

'Is he all right?' asked Lomond, holding out his spare keys.

'Yeah, he's fine,' Ross replied. 'I think he finds it funny. A good bit funnier than Isla will find it.'

'We can keep this between us if you'd prefer.'

'I appreciate it, boss. But I don't like keeping things from Isla. Always tell the truth. The easiest thing to remember, my mum always said.'

Lomond pushed his lips and nodded approvingly. 'Wise words.'

Ross opened the front door and put his arms out. 'Hey, I'm back!'

Lachlann came charging through from the living room, his arms outstretched too.

Ross laughed, preparing himself for impact. Only for Lachlann to go charging right past him, and out towards Lomond.

'You want uu-up!' Lachlann declared in a singsong voice, looking up at Lomond with puppy dog eyes.

Ross explained, 'He's still getting his you and I confused.'

'Oh yeah,' Lomond said, picking him up. '*I* knew what *you* meant. Didn't *I*?'

Lachlann broke into hearty laughter.

Lomond asked Ross, 'Are you coming in once you've dropped him off?'

'Yeah,' he replied.

'Good. Because Donna thinks she's got an ID on some of the kids in that Jimmy Gribbin photo. We need to knock on some doors today.'

Ross read between the lines. He said to Lachlann, 'Right, buddy. We had a wee adventure and now it's time to get to nursery.'

Lomond turned to leave. 'Right. See you soon.' He turned back to wave. 'Bye, Lachlann!'

Ross thought about leaving it, but thought it as good a time as any, given how rarely he and Lomond were left alone for any length of time. 'Sorry...John. Two seconds...'

Lomond trilled his lips before he turned around, sensing what was coming. 'I know what you're going to say, Ross.'

'About what?'

'It's fine, really. I appreciate Isla's attempts to set this date up with Catriona. And she seems like a lovely woman. But it's not a good time.' He turned to leave again, only for Ross to insist.

'See, I don't agree with that,' he said.

Lomond stopped once more.

Ross explained, 'I know it must be hard to think about starting–'

Lomond put his hands out in a defensive pose. 'Ross, let me

stop you there. You don't have the first clue about what I think about, all right. Have you thought about what it's like to love someone so much that you want to have children with them? And then you lose not only them, but...' He broke off. Not wanting to get into specifics in front of Lachlann. 'You lose everything, all at once. Maybe you're not supposed to recover from something like that.' He shrugged. 'Maybe it's just meant to hurt like hell. Imagine falling in love with someone while still loving someone who's no longer here. That's what I'm afraid of. Okay? It would be like I was cheating on Eilidh with every thought I ever had. And, you know, maybe there's only enough space in a heart for one other person.'

Ross replied, 'I don't believe that. Hearts are bigger than you think, John.'

Lomond exhaled, letting out months, even years, of pressure from the conflicted thoughts in his head. 'I had nightmares, Ross. For days, after I made plans with Catriona.'

'I never said it would be easy,' Ross replied. 'That doesn't mean you shouldn't do it.'

Lomond appreciated that Ross at least had the decency not to throw out something like "Eilidh would want you to be happy." Or something else that purported to speak for his dead wife.

His tone lowered by an octave. He was too tired to handle such a conversation so early in the morning. 'I need to get back to the office,' he said. When he reached his car, he told Ross, 'I'll think about it, okay.'

CHAPTER THIRTY-ONE

THE SOUND of Greggs paper wrappers and bags, and the smell of steak bakes, pies, and pepperoni pizza slices were redolent in the air of the MIT office.

Lomond recoiled from the smell, watching Jason with revulsion as he tucked into the pizza slice. 'Seriously, Jase? Pizza for breakfast?'

'I'm bulking,' Jason said with his mouth stuffed.

'Bulking?'

Jason had taken on too much to be able to say a word now.

Ross filled in for him. 'It means he's trying to put on weight.'

'You want to put on *more* weight? Son, you can bench press my car.'

Jason stifled laughter while he chewed enough down so he could respond. 'It's just a bit of lean mass, I'm after. On the plus side, I can eat whatever I want for a few weeks.'

Lomond looked intrigued. 'Whatever you want?' He clapped his hands. 'Right, folks, it's official. I am now bulking.'

Once the laughter died down, he added, 'But I still wouldn't eat a slice of pizza for breakfast. It's like taking food into the bathroom. It's just weird and wrong.' While the others tucked in to their food, Lomond held court in front of the whiteboard, where a blown-up version of the Boland Castle photograph was now front and centre. 'Good morning,' Lomond announced, pointing to the photo. 'This was taken on the grounds of Boland Castle hospital. This man at the centre is Jimmy Gribbin. Deceased. We need to corroborate the claims against Jimmy that he may have been involved in abuse of his daughter, Lianne. The connection to Boland Castle is, of course, a key part of this enquiry in establishing what other victims might be out there. Boland is at the heart of all of this now. So Donna and Ross, Pardeep and Jason...'

Willie handed out files to both pairings.

Lomond went on, 'We've now got identities of several of the children in this photograph. They need interviewed. We need to find out how involved Jimmy was with all of this. Was it just Lianne? Was it others as well? Did he use and abuse his position in the hospital for access to minors? And as Bob here will attest, that could open the door to a much bigger picture.' He paused to let his next point sink in. 'We could be looking at a network of abusers, from Boland Castle all the way up through the Scottish legal establishment.' He backed away to a table, where Lianne Gribbin's notebook was sitting, bagged as evidence. 'In this diary, Lianne documents many men coming and going to the hospital. It's consistent with everything Angela Devlin alleged in her abuse case before Lianne went missing. But we need evidence now. Names. Statements if you can get them. But be careful how hard you push. These are very sensitive interviews. Remember that you could be asking someone to relive the worst moments of their lives.' Lomond strode across to the board, pointing out a picture of Walter Murdock that had been found that morning, taken from his passport file. 'As for Walter, he's still in the wind. I'm hoping for more from forensics later today to get an ID on the blood found in the bathroom. Until then, me, Willie, and Bob are going to pay Bruce Murdock a visit in Edinburgh. If he has any evidence of an abuse network then we need to get it, and fast. As for Walter Murdock, provided the blood in the bathroom isn't actually his, then we've got traces on all of his bank accounts and cards, phone, and we've got number plate recognition starting as we speak. So hopefully we get a hit on Walter soon. That's it.'

As the team broke up into their pairs, they came together in the middle of the bullpen, comparing the files they had been given.

'What have you got?' asked Jason.

'Hugh Paterson,' Donna replied. 'You guys?'

Pardeep shuffled through the files. 'First up...Barry Jenkins. Lives in sheltered housing.'

Jason leaned over for a look. 'Govan. Cool. Not far.'

Lomond came over, clapping his hands to hustle them out the door. 'Come on, guys. Let's go. Busy day...'

Linda knocked on her window upstairs, holding her phone aloft, then gesturing towards Lomond's desk.

Lomond picked up his phone. 'Yeah?'

'Colin Mowatt's at reception for you.'

'Mowatt? Tell him he can wait until there's a press conference. We're not confirming any IDs on the bridge remains.'

'Do I look like your secretary, John?' She didn't wait for a response. 'He's not asking about the bridge remains. He's asking about Bruce Murdock.'

'Why on earth would he be asking about him?'

'Well, this is a wild suggestion, so take it with a pinch of salt. But maybe you could walk down two flights of stairs to find out?' She hung up on him.

CHAPTER THIRTY-TWO

At reception, a baby-faced man with floppy red hair and bright freckles was pacing around nervously, clutching a laptop bag.

'Hey,' said Lomond. 'It's Ron Weasley! What can I give you no comment on today?'

Mowatt wasn't laughing. In fact, he wasn't his usual self at all. Gone was the typical sneer and smirk wasn't there. Replaced with something Lomond had never seen on Mowatt's face before: a genuine sense of gravity and seriousness.

'DCI Lomond,' Mowatt began, holding out his hand.

Lomond looked at it with contempt. He couldn't easily forget some of the shit that Mowatt had slung at Police Scotland in recent times. For almost anyone else, he could have held his nose and shook hands to start off a polite footing. But not with Mowatt.

Lomond made a point of retracting his hand. 'No, I'm good, thanks.' He let it be known that Mowatt had only his bare minimum of attention, glancing over his head, as if the goings on in Bellahouston Park across the road held more interest for him.

Mowatt shook his head. 'I didn't come here to cause any trouble. Or to ask about the human remains that have been found at the Govan-Partick bridge construction site.'

Lomond rocked on his heels, still looking anywhere but at Mowatt's face. 'Good. Then why are you here?'

Mowatt let out a deep exhalation. Whatever he had to say, it appeared to be genuinely weighing heavily on his mind.

Slowly, Lomond got the feeling that something was going on. Something worth his time.

Mowatt stepped back, away from the reception desk to be out of earshot of the officer behind it. He lowered his voice further. 'Someone's reached out to us offering a story about a network of child abusers. And it involves someone I think you might currently be investigating.'

'What makes you say that?' asked Lomond.

'Well, that's confidential on my side,' Mowatt replied. 'But I've just spent the last two days sitting with a victim of this network. And Charlie too.'

Charlie Ferguson, editor of the *Glasgow Express*.

Lomond was no fan of the paper, but he at least respected Ferguson to the degree that any story he was willing to sit and listen to was also worth Lomond's time.

'Who's the victim?' asked Lomond.

'I can't reveal that. Not yet.' Seeing Lomond bristling, Mowatt held out a hand. 'Not *yet*, I'm saying. But they want someone from the police to listen to their story. They've specifically asked for you. And only you.'

'Look, Colin, I appreciate that this is a sensitive matter, whoever it involves. But there are levels to these things. And jumping straight to a DCI for something like this is skipping over several of those levels. So let me get you one of my best detective constables. Donna Higgins. You'll know her from the Sandman enquiry. She'll give you and your source everything you need.'

'No,' said Mowatt. 'This one's a dealbreaker, Detective Chief Inspector. This contact has attempted to report this to the police in the past. They've been quite clear. They speak only to you on this one.'

Lomond thought it over. 'Can you at least tell me who the allegations are against?'

Mowatt took a beat, anticipating that what he was about to say would rock Lomond's enquiry. 'The allegations are against Bruce Murdock KC.'

CHAPTER THIRTY-THREE

It took Donna and Ross two passes of Hugh Paterson's street in a dense Erskine housing estate before they realised they had found the right place. Almost every street was on a tight sweep, and the house and street markings were almost non-existent. Telling one building from another was a lottery.

'This is like the estate I grew up on,' said Donna.

'Me too,' said Ross.

The buildings were a mix of three-storey blocks with tiny square windows, and oppressively low bungalows. All with the same grey exterior, mixed with random wood panelling. A coda to seventies architecture that was dated before people even moved into them.

There were random traffic cones at various points along the pavement, where they would sit for years before anyone bothered to remove them – remnants of roadworks for laying broadband cables and repairing gas pipes over the years.

Curtains twitched as Donna and Ross approached the buzzer for Hugh's building. Everything about their appearance, their demeanour, screamed police to the locals. Little did they know the horrors that their unassuming neighbour was about to recount.

A slender, unshaven man wearing an unseasonably warm fleece opened the door.

'Hugh Paterson?' said Ross.

'That's me,' he replied. He had a soft, reedy voice, higher pitched than his tough, granite face suggested. The voice of a man who had been told a thousand times as a child to shut up and to disappear.

The flat was poky, furnished the way it had come from the previous tenant, a pensioner who had passed away in the hallway where they were discovered several days later. The place smelled of a million microwave meals and cups of builders' tea.

There was something incongruous about seeing a relatively young man such as Hugh – at thirty-eight years old – living in such a place.

Every room was tiny, and even Ross felt like he needed to stoop to avoid hitting his head on the doorframes.

Hugh led them into the living room, where he had set up three mugs along with a teapot and a separate pot of coffee, and a plate of Tesco's budget range of digestive biscuits. 'I'm a bit confused about what you think I can help you with.'

Donna and Ross shared a small two-seater snuggler. It was that or standing.

'Sorry I can't offer either of you this one,' said Hugh, sitting down in an armchair. 'I did my back in a few months ago. I've been on the sick for months now.'

'What happened?' asked Donna.

'I was working for a guy who builds self-assembly furniture. I was carrying a massive wardrobe panel up to a first-floor flat. I went to lean it against the wall, but it was top heavy. It pushed me back towards the bannister, but the weight was so much it tipped me right over the edge.'

Ross said, 'You fell over a first-floor rail?'

'Yeah. Landed flat on my back.' He picked up a bottle of prescription painkillers with a popular brand name on it. 'I've been munching these like Smarties. They don't do nothing to take the edge off.' He necked a few of the pills along with a glug of tea.

Still on edge from his debacle with Lachlann earlier that morning, Ross was in need of a strong coffee. He poured, while Donna asked.

'Mr Paterson, we–'

'You don't have to do that,' he said. 'Just Hugh.'

'Hugh,' Donna started again. 'We're currently investigating the identities of individuals in a photograph that's pertinent to an ongoing enquiry. Would you mind taking a look at it for us, please?'

Hugh seemed genuinely stumped about what he was about to be shown. But the second he saw it, his face crumpled from all four sides. 'Oh my god...' His mouth hung open, almost struggling for breath. 'Where...where did you find this?'

'I'm not at liberty to divulge that at this point, Hugh,' Donna explained. 'But could you take a look at the people in this photo. Is there anyone here you recognise.'

He scoffed. 'Of course there is.' He immediately pointed out the only adult in the shot. 'That's Jimmy.'

'Did you know his surname?' Ross asked.

'Sure. Jimmy Gribbin.'

'And do you recognise the location?'

Hugh let out a deep sigh. 'Recognise it? How could I forget the shit hole. It's Boland Castle.'

'Do you remember how long you were there for?'

'From the age of about three to sixteen.'

Ross couldn't mask his shock at the length of time.

Hugh said, 'There's people in and out of jail for murder in less time.'

'I didn't want to say,' said Donna.

'It's fine. I mean, it was basically a prison, anyway. A sort of open prison. They let you out the ward in the morning, then you had to be back for dinnertime. God help you if you weren't. The staff were brutal, man. Brutal.'

'Why were you there?' asked Donna.

Hugh shook his head, mystified. 'God knows. My birth mum let me go when I was a baby, then my foster parents dumped me in there. There was nothing wrong with me. It was meant to be a place for people with learning disabilities. I wasn't the only one like that. It was just a dumping ground for difficult kids. Rough kids, you know, that no one knew what to do with.'

Ross asked, 'What can you tell me about Jimmy Gribbin, Hugh?'

Hugh's expression softened. 'Jimmy was really nice. Probably the only nice one there. He saw what went on. He stepped in whenever he could, but the staff did whatever they wanted. They were all head cases themselves. Worse than the patients. We were in the middle of the countryside, with no one looking. No one checking. No inspections. We were just dirt on a shoe to the staff.'

'He was a sort of handyman at the hospital,' said Ross. 'Is that correct?'

'Yeah, but he was more than that. The kids liked him because he let us play with the horses.' Hugh pointed to the photo sitting next to the drinks tray. 'That one was Billy. Beautiful horse, so he was.'

'Why was Jimmy involved with horses at the hospital?'

'There were stables at the perimeter of the site, and apparently Jimmy wanted to be a jockey when he was young. But he said he was too tall. On his days off he used to teach kids how to ride.' While looking again at the horse, Hugh noticed a familiar face in the group. One of the children.

'Do you recognise someone else?' asked Donna.

He snorted. Somewhat derisively. 'Yeah. That was Barry. Barry Jenkins.'

'You don't sound impressed,' said Ross.

'Yeah. Weirdo. Total weirdo. Nobody liked him. To be fair, he was someone that was meant to be there. No' right in the head.'

'In what way?'

Hugh shook his head, struggling to find the right term. 'Just...in all ways. He was really into horses. Like, obsessed though.' He snorted as he remembered a story. 'There was one time, he was caught pulling himself off in the stables. That wasn't even the weirdest bit about it. He'd put on the bridle and the reins and everything over his head. He even put the metal...' He couldn't recall the terminology.

Ross offered, 'The bit?'

'Yeah, that goes in the horse's mouth. He was chewing down on that. I never seen it myself, but about four other kids found him.'

Ross pursed his lips, then stood up. He said softly, 'Could you excuse me a sec...'

He took his phone out casually, but inside he was panicking, his heart going a mile a minute. When he got into the hall, he called Pardeep as quick as he could. 'Come on, come on, come on...' he said hurriedly to himself, begging for an answer.

But there was no signal.

CHAPTER THIRTY-FOUR

PARDEEP AND JASON had no idea what they were walking into when they parked on Barry Jenkins' cul-de-sac. The pair had spent their whole careers going in and out of buildings far more dangerous and threatening than Barry's.

Jason had barely said a word since leaving Helen Street.

As Pardeep shut off the engine, he said, 'You all right?'

The question snapped him out of his daze. He hadn't even noticed how zoned out he had been.

'Yeah,' Jason said distantly, 'sorry.'

'It's obviously something. Spit it out, come on.'

Jason smiled. It was just like Pardeep to show that he cared by how irritated he clearly was at being kept waiting. 'I was thinking about how lucky I've been. You know, growing up. We didn't have a lot, but I was never hungry. No one kicked the crap out of me. And here we are, going to see this guy. He's lived in sheltered housing his whole adult life. He's, what, fifty-six? God knows he's never going to live unsupported anywhere. He's just been locked up pretty much his whole life.' Recalling the file on Barry, Jason said, 'From three until seventeen at Boland Castle. And now this.' He gestured at the rough-looking streets. Two separate gangs of neds were at each end, a few on scooters, wearing balaclavas. Some kicking a ball about in a casually threatening way. Shouting abuse at random strangers. 'I'll bet he doesn't get an easy time of it around here.'

'Not with his track record,' said Pardeep. 'You can't live around somewhere like this with a record and keep it quiet. There's always someone who knows a guy, who knows another guy, who did time with you. No secrets here.'

'I was just feeling grateful, that's all.'

Pardeep nodded. 'We're all right.'

Part of Pardeep's talents lay in reading between the lines. His bullshit detector had been carefully calibrated growing up. And he was sensing that Jason was feeling strange about talking to someone who might have been abused as a child. It wasn't in Pardeep's wheelhouse to give a speech to make Jason feel all right about it. Instead, he pivoted to what he knew best in pressure-filled times.

Jokes.

'You've got nothing to feel guilty about, Jase,' said Pardeep. 'It's just luck. That's all it is. Check it out, right. I was on the desk in Pollokshaws, when this guy calls in. Says his wife's missing. So I ran through the usual questions, you know. Can you describe her. He says, I don't know. Normal.' Pardeep chuckled. 'Normal, he says. So I ask what colour is her hair? He says, I don't know. It changes a lot. She called it burnt umber I think. I was, like, what are you talking about, mate? I've no idea what burnt umber is. So I ask what colour are her eyes. He must know that. He says I haven't really noticed...'

Jason's smile widened as the story progressed.

Pardeep continued, 'What's her weight roughly? He says

medium. Okay, what about her height? He says medium. Hair length, I says. He says?'

Jason chuckled as he answered. 'Medium?'

'Medium again, bro! I swear. This dude's got the most average wife in the world. So I move on from physical description, because I'm getting nowhere. I ask him, where did you last see her? He tells me she went out in his car. Okay, I says. What does the car look like? That's when his voice changes all hyper, and he tells me it's a V8 engine with six hundred horsepower, does zero to sixty in three point two seconds, with plush seats, and alloys that have this subtle curve to the grills...I swear, Jason, mate, the dude bangs on about his car for the next two minutes straight. I had to remind the guy his wife was missing.'

Jason was folded over with laughter.

It wasn't even true. It was a joke that had been passed down through the station from two different generations of officer before him. But its truth wasn't the point. It had made Jason laugh, and forget about everything he had been worrying about.

'Come on,' Pardeep said. 'Let's go.'

They hit the buzzer for Barry Jenkins' flat, initially getting a reply but he then failed to buzz the detective constables in. They were too late in the day to use the services buzzer. It took repeatedly buzzing the neighbours to get access to the building.

'What do you think that's about?' asked Jason.

Pardeep wasn't remotely worried. 'Who knows.'

'He definitely answered, didn't he?'

'Don't worry about it, Jase.'

They stopped outside Barry's door. Pardeep knocked hard. Twice. 'Police, Mr Jenkins. Can you open the door?'

The door opened gently. Only enough to let a tiny sliver of light in, illuminating a thin channel of Barry Jenkins' face.

'Hello?' he said.

Pardeep showed his ID, as did Jason.

'Mr Jenkins, I'm Detective Sergeant Pardeep Varma. This is my colleague Detective Constable Jason Yang. We're here to ask you a few questions.'

Barry moved to close the door. 'No, thank you. Sorry.'

Pardeep put his hand on the door to stop it from closing. 'We're here about Boland Castle. Do you remember?'

Barry let go of the door.

'You do remember it,' Pardeep said.

'Yes,' Barry replied softly.

Pardeep took out a copy of the photograph to show him, then indicated Jimmy Gribbin. 'We're trying to find out some information about this man. Do you know him?'

'That's Jimmy.'

Pardeep held his gaze a long time, unwavering. There was something about Barry's demeanour that threw up a red flag. 'Do you think we could come in for a few minutes, Barry? Is that all right?' Pardeep took one step inside, waiting for resistance that never came.

Jason followed quickly behind.

But Barry stayed rooted to the spot by the door, holding it open. He was staring at the ground.

'Are you all right, Barry?' Jason asked.

'You said you had some questions?'

'That's right,' said Pardeep, taking out his notepad.

Jason stayed where he was, but had a good look about the place. It was a tip. Dry rubbish everywhere. Tons of sweet wrappers and crisp packets. All left on the floor.

The hallway was in almost complete darkness, as the curtains had been closed in every room, and the only light source in the flat was the TV.

It was playing at a deafening volume in the living room.

Some daytime show, talking about a lot of nothing for four hours Monday to Friday. Barry liked those shows because they kept him company.

Pardeep indicated towards the TV. 'I'm sorry, Barry. Could you maybe turn that down a bit so we can hear each other a little better?'

Barry marched straight off as if he had been given an instruction by an army drill sergeant.

While he was gone, Jason tapped Pardeep on the side.

Pardeep flicked his head up, asking '*what?*'

Jason used his foot to indicate the empty cardboard box on the floor.

The one from the equestrian website that clearly had horse branding on it.

Pardeep's eyes widened. He called through to Barry, who was taking his time to return, even though he had turned the TV down already. 'Barry...is there anyone else in the flat? Anyone we should be aware of?'

Barry returned to the hall and shook his head. 'No.'

The pair were relieved to hear it, but they wouldn't believe it until they knew for sure.

'Can we see the other room, please, Barry?' Pardeep asked.

Barry returned to the hall, then walked straight past the officers. He pushed his bedroom door open. Then the bathroom. Then a cupboard door next to the kitchen. And the kitchen had no door.

While Jason inspected the bedroom from the doorway, satisfied that it was empty, Pardeep went inside, opening the wardrobe's sliding doors. He froze as he noticed blood stains on the wall inside. Pardeep stepped aside and pointed it out to Barry. 'Has someone been hurt in here?'

'I never hurt them,' Barry said. 'I'm saving them. Setting them free. I give them the reins to guide them.'

Jason, focusing on what Pardeep had found, stood with his back to Barry. When he whipped around after hearing Barry's words, it was too late to react. Before he saw the blade, it plunged deep into his side.

Pardeep cried out, "No!" and lunged towards Barry, disregarding his own safety as Barry drew the knife back for another strike. Pardeep threw up a defensive arm, deflecting the blade away from Jason but into the left side of his own torso.

Barry twisted the knife, trying to release it. Pardeep let out a guttural groan from the searing agony. Now his defences were down, and blood was pouring out of his stomach.

As Jason slid out of Barry's grasp and onto the floor, Pardeep fell onto his back, arms at his sides. He had no defences as Barry straddled him, raising the knife high and plunging it into Pardeep's heart.

The moment it pierced him, Pardeep knew he was done for. Few people survive a knife to the heart. Pardeep didn't need a medical opinion to know that he was dying.

Jason, slipping into semi-consciousness, reached out for his colleague. Realising Pardeep was too far, he grabbed his handcuffs. Mouth open in a silent scream, only air and blood came out.

Helpless, he watched Barry withdraw the blade from Pardeep's chest, releasing a geyser of blood. Pardeep's body jolted, like he'd been given an electric shock. Then his head fell to one side.

Barry turned to get up, stunned to find Jason clutching his wound with one hand and holding open handcuffs with the other. Jason whipped the sharp end of the cuffs across Barry's face, slicing his cheek, then dropped an elbow onto Barry's face, knocking him out instantly.

For safety, Jason rushed to get cuffs on him while Barry's legs jerked and twitched from the impact of the elbow strike.

Jason tapped Pardeep's face, trying to wake him up. 'Pardeep! Hey! Listen to me, you're going to be okay. You hear me?...'

He tried to remove a hand from his wound to aid his immobile colleague. But the moment he released pressure, blood gushed through his fingers like a dam breaking.

Jason started to cry. With only one hand, he was helpless.

'Please, Pardeep, don't die on me, man...come on...'

He laid his phone on the floor and called 999. 'I'm DC Jason Yang of Helen Street MIT. I need urgent assistance. I've got an officer stabbed in the chest...'

Only then did Jason realise the full extent of Pardeep's injuries. And that he was most probably already dead.

He gave the operator Barry Jenkins' address, and did what he could with one hand. But he couldn't stand it any longer. He wasn't going to let Pardeep die because he couldn't take some pain.

Although it was much more than just that.

It was ten out of ten on the pain scale.

Insufferable. Impossible pain.

But he grimaced and put himself through it all the same. After just a few seconds, his head felt light. Still, Jason attempted a combination of CPR and to cover the chest wound. He didn't care if it cost him his own life. He wasn't going to let his colleague go down.

He battled valiantly while the operator talked him through it. He kept going until his vision darkened, knowing he would pass out.

The operator called out to him for a response, but Jason lay inert, unconscious on Pardeep's chest.

The operator assured him, 'Officers have your address, DC Yang. Stay with me...Do you hear me? Stay with me...'

CHAPTER THIRTY-FIVE

LOMOND AND WILLIE sat in front of Charlie Ferguson's desk in the editor's office of the *Glasgow Express* – by some distance, the nicest, biggest office in the newsroom. Bob Torrance was also there, but had decided to stand by the floor-to-ceiling window, taking in the view.

Located at Anderston Quay, where the River Clyde passed under the Kingston Bridge, it felt like enemy territory for Lomond. He'd had his share of run-ins with Mowatt there and elsewhere. But this time felt different.

The newsroom was quiet, even for a midweek morning. Too soon since the previous day's edition, and too long to go until the next one, reporters rested on their laurels, feeling like they had all the time in the world.

Lomond asked over his shoulder, 'What do you think, Bob?'

Torrance considered the options. 'I don't know what to think anymore.'

Willie suggested, 'If it's true, then this conspiracy theory stuff about paedophile judges and cops must be bollocks.'

'Must it?' wondered Lomond.

Torrance said, 'The CPS destroyed Bruce Murdock's case prosecuting the men who groomed and abused Angela Devlin. That's what started this whole thing. This could be an establishment inside job to discredit the one man who has a list of the most powerful people in the country who are involved in a network of grooming and abuse.'

'Says who?'

The question seemed to stump Torrance.

'I'm serious,' said Lomond. 'Why are we supposed to take it on face value?'

The office flew open, and in strode Charlie Ferguson, editor of the *Express*. 'Gents,' he said, in a hard Glaswegian accent. 'You're supposed to take it on face value, DCI Lomond, because it came from Bruce Murdock. And he had grown accustomed to people swallowing his shit. Murdock is the biggest bullshit artist that the Scottish legal system has known – as is about to be demonstrated.'

Torrance sat down beside Lomond and Willie. 'I'm all ears, Charlie.'

He poured himself a whisky from the bar area in the corner. He held the bottle aloft, offering one to the others.

Lomond pointed out, 'It's not even eleven, Charlie.'

'That's the beauty of being editor. No one's going to stop me.'

'As long as you're not planning on getting behind the wheel of that lovely Jag anytime soon.'

Charlie took up a position behind his desk, standing tall. 'Before we get started here, gents, I want to assure you that I've put my absolute best behind this one.'

'Colin Mowatt?' Willie sniped.

Charlie smiled. 'Okay, you got me there. He's just the face of this. And when you hear the story, you're going to be glad of it. Because with Colin's national exposure these days, this story's going to be at the top of the news agenda for a while.'

Lomond looked around. 'Where is the little bam, anyway?'

'He's sitting with his source next door in Colin's office. They'll be through shortly. But before they join us, I'm telling you that this thing has been vetted upways, sideways, and inside out. Not by Colin, but by a dedicated fact-checking team. Everything Colin's source has told me, and is about to tell you, has been verified, and corroborated by a second source.'

'Double-stamped?' Lomond said in surprise.

'Trust me, John. On a story like this, I wouldn't do anything else. A story like this goes wrong, it can shutter a paper for good.'

Lomond wasn't mad about what Charlie Ferguson stood for. Which was the Wild West, when it came to news. He might have been cavalier, but he wasn't a bullshit artist. He'd cut his teeth on some of the best broadsheets in Fleet Street over a multi-decade career. If he said he trusted a story, then Lomond was inclined to give him the benefit of the doubt.

Charlie hit the intercom on his phone. 'You can come in now,' he said.

A few seconds later, Colin Mowatt exited his office, then waited for his source to appear behind.

Lomond, Willie, and Torrance all leaned back in their chairs to get an earlier glimpse of who the source was.

When they finally appeared, it set off a wave of exclamations from the officers.

'Well, fuck me...'

'Christ, of course...'

'Aw, bloody hell...'

Mowatt held the door open, then in stepped Walter Murdock, whose expression was somewhere between that of a man on the way to the firing squad, and a man desperate to tell his story.

Murdock took a seat alongside Ferguson's desk on the far side, with Mowatt and Ferguson flanking him.

Lomond noted that Murdock's hands were trembling. 'Charlie tells us you have a story to tell us, son.'

Walter nodded. 'I do.'

He was wearing a shirt with no tie under a double-breasted blazer that looked more expensive than most of the cars Lomond had owned in his lifetime. He was well spoken. A quiet voice that forced you lean forward to pay attention.

Lomond said, 'I think it's fair to say we have a lot of questions over on this side of the room. But why don't you tell us what you've told Charlie and Colin so far.'

Walter cleared his throat, needing two attempts. 'From the age of around five years old, I was sexually abused by my father, Bruce Murdock, KC, and a number of his closest associates. The abuse started in my childhood home in Edinburgh, where my father still resides. And continued even when I was sent off to Boland Castle hospital at the age of ten. Boland Castle, as I will detail, was ground zero for a network of child abusers and groomers, who preyed on vulnerable children, plying us with booze and drugs to keep us compliant, and using their vast web of power and influence to prevent the authorities ever taking action against them. By any other name, Boland Castle was a prison. Until one night in the late nineties, a teenager named Angela Devlin managed to escape. When she ends up in a position to name the men who had abused her in that flat in Edinburgh, the network closed ranks, and sent in one of their own to protect the network.'

Lomond said, 'So the network is real.'

'Yes,' Walter replied. 'Very much so.'

'Walk me through how it worked, Walter. What did your dad do, and how?'

'That was simple. He started a rumour – a false rumour, as it turns out – about a judge. Angela Devlin had never met Lord Windermere in her life–'

Willie began, 'But how–'

'How do I know that? Because my father told me. He was desperate to tell me and anyone who would listen, how clever he had been. When Angela went to the police, the network had a real problem. It doesn't take long for this to feed back to those at the very heights of the Scottish legal system. That's when my father has an idea. He tells them to put him forward as prosecution QC. He then starts the rumour about Windermere, apparently working in Angela Devlin's interests. When the whole time, unknown to her, my father was conspiring to help the very men who had abused her. The rumour is enough to collapse the trial. All of my father's associates walk free.'

'It's a compelling story, Walter, but to be rather brutally selfish about things, there's a ton of evidence linking you to two women who have been murdered in very similar fashion.'

Walter said, 'You're talking about Tricia Dunn and Lianne Gribbin, right?'

'I am.'

After thinking through his wording, Walter said, 'Ever since I was ten years old, I've been dreaming of the day that the men who abused me, and so many others in Boland Castle, would one day see justice. Thanks to the inheritance left by my mother, I've dedicated all the resources at my disposal to find other victims, and encourage them to break ground and press charges. Unfortunately, the police proved themselves as susceptible to corruption as those who aided my father through the years. Whether as part of an intentional desire to help abusers get away with their crimes. Or just good old-fashioned corruption and manipulation to do favours for powerful men.'

Lomond asked, 'And what about the blood we found in your bathroom?'

Walter looked down and away. For the first time, he appeared evasive. 'No comment.'

Willie and Lomond shared a quick look with one another.

They had an idea what the response meant, but they wouldn't know for sure until the police got to Bruce Murdock's flat in Edinburgh's New Town.

Lomond rose first. 'Walter, needless to say this is going to be the first of many conversations we're going to have. Thank you for trusting us to do this right this time.' He offered Walter his hand. 'We're going to do everything we can to bring these men to justice.'

As Walter shook Lomond's hand, he told him, 'I've already secured justice.'

Lomond nodded. 'Aye. That's what I was afraid of, son. I really hope for your sake you haven't done what I think you have.'

'Sometimes,' Walter said, 'you have to do whatever it takes to close a certain door, so that another one can open up.'

On their way back to the car, Lomond noticed Torrance trailing behind, his head hanging lower than usual. 'You all right, Bob?'

Torrance replied, 'I've sacrificed a lot to hear what I just did up there. It gets to a point where you start to think you might actually be crazy.'

Lomond told him, 'If one person tells you that you're

drunk, they might be wrong. If the entire room tells you that you're drunk, then it's probably time to go home. You were right not to listen to all those voices. Without you, Tricia Dunn would just be another cold case.'

'And now you're done, right?' Willie checked.

Torrance smiled. 'Oh, I'm done all right. I dunno what the wife will make of that though.'

Lomond answered his phone, still smiling from the exchange. But the smile soon vanished when Linda relayed to him what had just happened at Barry Jenkins' flat.

CHAPTER THIRTY-SIX

THE HOSPITAL HAD LAID out Pardeep's body in a private viewing room near the mortuary. His body had been cleaned, and bore no visible signs of the trauma he had endured.

Lomond stood over the body, shoulders trembling as tears rattled out of him. He laid his hand on top of Pardeep's.

Even now, after touching so many dead bodies, the coldness still took him by surprise. The depth of it. And how quickly the colour grey can take over a body. The jaw pulled hard at either side, giving in to gravity, muscles slackening.

But to Lomond, he was still Detective Constable Pardeep Varma. And always would be.

'I'm sorry, son,' Lomond cried.

Outside, Willie sat in a wooden chair, having already paid his respects. He had taken the news hard, having been the one to hand out the files that sent Pardeep and Jason to Barry Jenkins.

'Any word on Jason?' Lomond asked.

'How long do you think you were in there?' said Willie.

Lomond let it go. Everyone's nerves were fraught. Tension was high.

Lomond crouched down to put his arm around Willie, who began to sob.

'His kids were just along the corridor...If I hadn't given him the file...If maybe I'd been the one to go...I've lived a life already...'

'You can't think like that,' Lomond told him, rubbing his back hard. 'Hey, come on. It wasn't your fault. It wasn't anybody's fault but Barry Jenkins.'

'Where is he anyway?'

'Undergoing psych evaluation at Helen Street.'

'If he walks, I'll never live with myself.'

'He won't walk,' Lomond assured him. 'I promise you that.' He patted Willie on the back. 'Come on. Let's go upstairs and see Jason.'

In the Intensive Care Unit in Glasgow's Queen Elizabeth Hospital, Jason was hooked up to more tubes and pumps than seemed either necessary or possible.

Lomond and Willie weren't allowed in to the room while doctors ran another plethora of tests.

Willie said, 'A shame he's not got anyone here waiting for him, poor sod. He should have got himself a bird by now.' Realising his modern faux pas, he corrected himself, 'Or, you know, a nice bloke. I don't the kid well enough. You know how some of them are the muscly types. They wear those tight t-shirts to show off their muscles...'

Lomond had put off interrupting as long as he could. 'Willie, what in god's name are you talking about?'

'I'm just saying, I'd feel better if the kid had someone standing here waiting for him to come around.'

'He does,' Lomond said. 'He's got us.'

The consultant came out of the room, holding a clipboard.

'How's he looking, doc?' Lomond asked.

She said, 'Well, we've managed to stabilise him. But he's suffered significant blood loss. What we call haemorrhagic shock. This can lead to critical drops in blood pressure and reduced oxygen delivery to vital organs, such as the brain. Which is why he's ended up in a coma.'

'What's the prognosis?' asked Willie.

The consultant shook her head gently. 'It's much too soon to tell. But we are hopeful of a recovery.'

'Recovery,' Lomond fired back quickly. 'How full a recovery?'

'Again, it's much too soon to know. The paramedics at the scene think he had been unconscious for longer than you would ever want. For what it's worth, they found Jason slumped on top of Mr Varma. It appears he was attempting to administer CPR to Mr Varma before succumbing to his own significant blood loss. If there are medals for withstanding pain, Jason would be a prime candidate for one.'

Once the consultant went back into the room, Lomond laid a hand on Willie's shoulder. 'Come on. Let's see what Barry Jenkins has to say.'

CHAPTER THIRTY-SEVEN

There was a lot that Lomond could complain about with Police Scotland. But what couldn't be faulted was the speed with which the Edinburgh police reached Bruce Murdock's flat in the New Town.

The residence was just around the corner from Charlotte Square. One of the most expensive and exclusive locations in the city. The First Minister's official residence, Bute House, was just a stone's throw away. And from the outside, there was little to separate it from Murdock's plush townhouse.

Officers, operating on instructions of imminent threat to life from Lomond, were expecting to find a dead body in the property. And judging by the amount of blood found in Walter Murdock's bathroom, a grisly, messy crime scene.

Once they had broken the door down, officers ran from room to room in search of Bruce.

Then the first officer in called out in shock when he reached Murdock's private study. 'He's...he's in here...' He then added a request which no one had been expecting.

'Medic!' he shouted. 'Medic!'

The other officers followed in swiftly behind.

Bruce Murdock was sitting upright in his office chair, stripped to his underwear, with a balled-up sock in his mouth, and his hands tied behind his back.

At his feet was a pool of blood, still dripping from the wounds in his chest. And his forehead.

The first officer stood helplessly in front of him. 'What the hell do I do?'

His colleagues crowded around him.

'Bloody hell...'

'What the...'

Murdock let out a cry of anguish, as far as he could with the sock in his mouth.

The officer took it out, which came as a huge relief to Murdock.

'What's he done?' Murdock spluttered. 'The little bastard... I'll kill him. I'll kill him. What did he write, the swine?'

The officer tending to him gulped hard, then turned to his senior officer for guidance. 'What do we do?'

The senior officer took one look at him. 'There's nothing we can do. Paramedics are on the way up.' He then said pointedly to Murdock. 'I wouldn't expect they can do very much for you.'

On Murdock's naked torso, were a dozen names carved into his skin with a knife. Names taken from Tricia Dunn's Beware Book. In the end, she had decided against going to the police with Walter Murdock. But she had given him the book for safe-keeping.

One officer remarked, 'That's one way of keeping a hard copy. Bloody hell...'

Not that they knew what the names were. But once the dust had settled in a few days, word would soon spread about one particular name carved into Murdock's chest.

Brendan Niven. Current Assistant Chief Constable.

But Walter had saved the most savage carving for his father's forehead.

Using a Stanley knife, the clean blade guaranteed that the scar left behind would be clearly legible until Bruce's dying day.

Across his forehead was the unmistakable word:

PAEDO

CHAPTER THIRTY-EIGHT

The psych evaluation for Barry Jenkins had concluded that he was of sound mind to be interviewed by legal counsel. A tortuous affair for the members of Major Investigations, whose eyes were still red with tears at the loss of Pardeep.

No one knew yet how culpable Barry Jenkins really was. Which made it difficult to attach their anger to him yet. Was it the work of someone mentally ill? Or a calculated killing out of self-preservation?

The lawyer removed his glasses as he exited the interview room. His expression was solemn, fully aware of the raw emotions in the air.

'What's he saying?' Lomond asked.

The lawyer took in a deep breath, as if he was out of his depth. 'Well, the doctors have declared him to be of sound mind. However, it's not quite as simple as the events suggest.'

'I've got a dead officer in the mortuary, son, and another lying in a coma because of your client. There's receipts in his flat going back six years which can be tied to the horse bridle and bit found on Tricia Dunn's body. And given the similarity to Lianne Gribbin's murder, you can be damn sure we'll be tying those two together with a bow for the CPS. So your guy had better start talking.'

The lawyer scoffed. 'Getting him to talk hasn't been an issue. He's had quite a bit to say. Namely, that he is not responsible for any murders of women. Or anyone else, for that matter.'

'If I can be frank with you, on a professional level, son,' said Lomond, 'I would urge you to change your client's position on that. Because there's not a jury in the land–'

The lawyer raised his hands defensively. 'Mr Jenkins has told me he was under the impression that he was saving the women. To use his phrase, he was "setting them free".'

'What's he mean by that?'

'I'm no expert, but I would suggest at a point in early life he became unnaturally obsessed with horses. He's spoken of a first sexual act taking place around one when he was a boy...' The lawyer trailed off, wondering how best to tackle the next topic. 'When discussing this childhood event, he also mentioned his brother. Peter. He claims Peter regularly engaged in sexual activity with him when they were both children. Activity which continued deep into their teens. Barry has stated that he never considered this activity consensual on his behalf. He's also mentioned similar activity that took place with minors both male and female during visits to Boland Castle. It was during this time that Peter developed, according to my client, a desire to commit murder. An act that my client repeatedly stopped Peter from engaging in. But it appears that Peter has been using Barry to capture women off the street. Peter then allows Barry to dress up the women with the horse reins, as part of his ritual of saving them from their lives on the street. In short, Chief Inspector–'

Lomond corrected him, 'Detective Chief Inspector, thanks.'

The lawyer bowed a little in apology. 'Barry Jenkins is the victim of an extremely dangerous and violent man, whose cruelty is matched only by his ability to manipulate a vulnerable and entirely innocent man. A man, who I might remind you, has suffered some of the worst abuse I've ever heard of.'

Lomond rubbed his face hard, not sure what to believe. Was it a cunning ploy to evade justice? Or the truth?

The lawyer went on, 'Barry also mentioned a garage lock-up in the Southside. He suggests your officers have a look inside. Apparently Peter had Barry snatch a girl only last week. But he claimed to Peter that the girl had escaped. He had in fact hidden her away in his flat since then.'

'Where is she now?'

The lawyer winced. 'He isn't sure.'

Lomond took out his notepad. 'Where's this lock-up?'

CHAPTER THIRTY-NINE

PETER JENKINS ARRIVED at the lock-up, making sure to turn his headlights off. He was in a secluded lane, but he wasn't taking any chances. The lock-up wasn't wide enough for a car to reverse into, so there had to be at least a few metres where the woman in his boot would be out in the open.

But the moment he opened the boot of his battered Ford, police lights lit up the surrounding industrial buildings. Painting the night sky blue.

Kicking and screaming for her life in the boot was a woman who had been abducted off the streets just half an hour earlier. Without Barry around to hold him back, there was no telling what would have become of her.

BACK AT HELEN STREET, while Peter Jenkins sat sombrely in the interview room, doubling down with ridiculous denials, Lomond stared at him through the one-way glass.

The face of a psychopath and malevolently evil man.

Willie joined him, handing him a machine coffee.

'Ta,' Lomond said.

'What's he saying?'

'Bugger all. Denials. No comment. He's going to sign his own life sentence with them.'

'Guess what I just heard from Lennoxtown?'

'What?' asked Lomond.

'A few hours ago, a dog walker found a woman wrapped up in horse reins in the middle of a field near Boland Castle. She said that two men had taken her. One of them had rescued her from the other one, then left her in the field. It seems Barry's story checks out.'

'I'll be damned,' said Lomond. He took a sip of coffee, then recoiled from the scalding heat of it. 'There go my tastebuds for the next three days. Fuck me...'

Willie said, 'Ross broke the news about finding Lianne's killer to Thomas Rafferty.'

'That was nice of him,' Lomond said. 'Can't say I'd have done the same.'

'Well, turns out, Rafferty's snatch of that woman was some stupid attempt to find information about Lianne. He didn't want to say, because Lianne had told him about some network of police and lawyers who had abused her at Boland Castle.'

'He was trying to find her killer,' said Lomond.

'In a dumb ass, terrifying way for the poor lassie.'

Willie nodded in the direction away from the interview room. 'Hey, we're going to grab a drink down the road. For Pardeep.'

'Sounds good.' But Lomond still hung back.

'Hey, John. We got him. It's over.'

Lomond nodded. 'I know.'

Once Willie was gone, Lomond took out his phone and sent a text.

In his house in Bearsden, Bob Torrance was busy carrying boxes out to his garage, ready to be returned to Helen Street.

He was in the process of putting a box down when he heard his phone ping with a message.

It was from Lomond.

"Enjoy retirement, boss."

Torrance stood back at his front door, thinking of the decades of work that had gone into combing through all the paperwork. And how, finally, all the hard work had paid off.

Now he was free to go upstairs with his wife. Where he belonged.

When he got to her bedside, he rubbed her hand.

'Okay, love?' he asked.

She tilted her head in such a way that let him know that she was.

'I'm here now,' he said. 'I'm done. For good this time.'

Still very weak, she squeezed his hand harder than she had in years.

CHAPTER FORTY

THE PUB on Paisley Road West was one of the rougher ones around, but the Major Investigations Team weren't looking for atmosphere and good food. They just needed to be in a room together somewhere that wasn't the property of Police Scotland.

Gathered around a small table, Lomond raised his glass of neat whisky. 'Pardeep, this one's for you, son.'

Donna, Ross, and Willie raised their glasses too, then they all downed their drinks.

'I can't stay too long,' Donna warned them.

'How come?'

'I need to be up early tomorrow.'

'What for?' Lomond asked.

'I need to deliver on a promise I made to Brenda Gribbin.'

Willie, already a bit the worse for wear, retreated to the bar along with his Ross.

While they were alone, Lomond told Donna, 'You were right, you know. To make that promise to her.'

'Oh yeah?' she replied. 'Why's that?'

Lomond nodded slowly to himself. 'Because hope is important. Hope...is what gets you through the next day. And the day after that. It's what tells you it might not always feel like this.'

'Thanks, boss,' Donna said, accepting a squeeze from Lomond's hand.

As the main door opened, Ross saw the reflection of someone he recognised in the mirror behind the bar.

'What the hell?' He went over to say hi. 'Catriona,' he announced, shaking his head in confusion. 'What are you doing here?'

She looked around nervously. 'I didn't actually know you were going to be here.' When she caught Lomond's eye, she raised her head with a smile.

'Yeah, great,' said Ross, bringing over more drinks to a table that was far too small.

Lomond stood up and offered a hand to Catriona, then they both laughed and fumbled their way through an embrace.

As she let go, she told Lomond, 'Isla told me earlier about what happened with your colleague. I'm so sorry, John.' She left her hand touching his arm.

He was surprised to find that he didn't find it awkward or unpleasant. 'Thanks. Yeah, it's been a tough day. I, eh...I know it might seem strange to reach out now, but I just thought... there's something about someone dying that makes you think about the future. You know?'

She nodded deeply. 'I do. I really do.'

Lomond looked towards the ceiling as a new song came on. 'I always loved this,' he said.

Even in middle age, there remained few feelings as gratifying as when a certain song comes on at just the right time.

Catriona paused, listening for a few seconds. 'I don't know it. What is it?'

'The Waterboys. "This is the Sea". Seems somehow appropriate.'

'Oh yeah? In what way?'

'The sea that he sings about...it's sort of about this vast, boundless future full of possibilities. It's about letting go of all your old ways. Embracing new beginnings. He sings about all the trouble, all the bad stuff, well, that was the river. But all this new stuff over here, that's the sea. And isn't that a beautiful thing?'

ALSO BY ANDREW RAYMOND

Novak and Mitchell

1. Official Secrets

2. Capitol Spy

3. Traitor Games

4. True Republic

DCI John Lomond – a Scottish crime series

1. The Bonnie Dead

2. The Shortlist

3. The Bloody, Bloody Banks

Duncan Grant

1. Kill Day

2. Dead Flags

Standalone

The Limits of the World

Printed in Great Britain
by Amazon